Lone star lover?

Matt stopped dead in his tracks. Facing him was a life-size poster of himself, suspended from the ceiling—and surrounded by women!

It wasn't his birthday. He hadn't been promoted. Dreaming seemed unlikely. And because he was standing inside the door of the Hole In The Wall bar, he knew he hadn't died and gone to heaven. He blinked, but the roomful of women watching him expectantly remained solid and real. Then, as if they'd seen a signal, they all started talking at once.

"Matt?"

"Mr. Travis?"

"Matthew…"

There were short ones, tall ones, plump ones, skinny ones, blondes, brunettes and redheads. The mix of several different varieties of perfume nearly smothered him. A city-bred blonde with a microphone maneuvered through the crowd followed by a cameraman. Her smile, not to mention her legs, could have given a lesser man heart palpitations.

"So, Mr. Tall, Dark and Reckless," Dee Cates said, seeming to enjoy his predicament. "How do you feel about the response to your ad?"

Dear Reader,

Coming from the South, I understand how history and tradition still play a role in the present day. When I first decided to make my hero a Texas Ranger, I knew the history. Now all I had to do was take a trip to Texas and track down the modern version. And was I ever glad that I did.

Texas Rangers are true heroes. The "top cops" in Texas, they are self-motivated, tenacious and dedicated. They are also, in most cases, family men.

So how, you ask, could the hero of *Tall, Dark and Reckless,* Ranger Matt Travis, end up with his picture in *Texas Men* magazine? Through the efforts of his practical joking friends, of course. Matt's buddies in law enforcement are determined to marry him off. So they decided to invite forty or so women to a party, with Matt, the Lone Star Lover, as the guest of honor.

Single-and-loving-it television reporter Dee Cates is thoroughly enjoying the Lone Star Lover's predicament— until he turns his killer grin and Texas charm in her direction. Then it's all she can do to remind herself to put business before pleasure.

I hope you enjoy a little Texas heat.

Happy Reading,

Lyn Ellis

Lyn Ellis
TALL, DARK AND RECKLESS

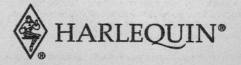

HARLEQUIN®

TORONTO • NEW YORK • LONDON
AMSTERDAM • PARIS • SYDNEY • HAMBURG
STOCKHOLM • ATHENS • TOKYO • MILAN • MADRID
PRAGUE • WARSAW • BUDAPEST • AUCKLAND

To Ranger Matt Cawthon, a true professional and a gentleman. Thanks for your help and for taking what I do seriously.

To the other 105 Texas Rangers: Don't be too hard on Matt. He only answered my questions. I made the rest up. <grin>

ISBN 0-373-25807-0

TALL, DARK AND RECKLESS

Printed in U.S.A.

_____ Prologue _____

THE AD COPY READ:

> LONE STAR LOVER—Dallas oilman prefers
> to live on his ranch in South Central Texas.
> Big-game hunter, raises exotic animals and
> quarter horses. Looking for a down-home
> Texas girl who can look past all that oil
> money and love him for the sensitive man he
> is.

The man in the ad standing next to a red Porsche
was handsome enough to star in his own soap
opera—"The Tall, the Dark and the Reckless."
Caught by the daredevil sparkle in eyes shaded
by the brim of a tan Stetson, Dee Cates read the ad
again and shook her head. Too bad. The guy definitely had fantasy potential and, considering his
ad, a towering, Texas-size ego.

Timberrrrrrr, she thought wickedly. The taller
they are, the harder they fall.

She might be the only unmarried reporter at
television station KAUS, in Austin, but even
she'd never resort to answering an ad in _Texas
Men Magazine_ for a date. Even if she had time for
one. She turned a few more pages. Picture after

picture of "eligible" men smiled at her with varying degrees of persuasiveness. *These guys are too much.* She chuckled. Did they really think they'd find the perfect woman by putting an ad in a magazine? Or, did they consider it a sport, like fishing? Bait the hook and see what, or who in this case, takes a bite.

She hoped they'd been inoculated for rabies.

Well, deluded or not, she needed to interview one or two of these "sportsmen" for the last segment of her feature on dating in the nineties. And since she didn't have the time or stamina to meet them all, she had to choose.

The phone rang. Without taking her gaze from the latest crop of possible interviewees, Dee picked up the receiver. "Cates."

"Have you chosen your next victim yet?" The voice belonged to Jim, her program director.

"*My* next victim? Do you realize that because of you, I'm still getting E-mail from CYBERSTUD in Lubbock? Not to mention phone calls from the manager of the Dating Corral." She sat back and picked up her diet cola. "If I didn't know better, I'd think you were trying to fix me up."

"You know I wouldn't do that to you," he said, sounding totally insincere. "I thought you'd be the perfect person to really *tune into* a single woman's perspective."

"So you've thrown me to the wolves?"

"Now, Dee…"

She'd attended several co-workers' weddings in the five years she'd worked at the station, including his, without suffering a twinge of envy. He was probably starting to wonder about her. She took a sip of her drink then set it back on her desk. "So what if I'm the only single reporter left on staff. It's not that I don't like men, I'm just not interested in marriage."

"But, Dee—"

She laughed. "I have a great job and a *wonder-*ful boss, what do I need a man for?"

"You need at least one more man to finish this piece. So, back to my original question, have you decided who?"

"Um..." Having lost her concentration, Dee flipped the magazine pages back to the beginning and started over. "Maybe," she hedged. "You'll be the first to know."

Hanging up the phone, she found herself staring at the Lone Star Lover once again. Her smile faltered. Goose bumps rose on her arms, making her skin feel electric. It wasn't the fancy car in the photo, or the sexy grin modeled by the man who looked like a young Clint Eastwood that affected her. It was the deserted location that jogged a memory. The lake and the hills in the background. And that crooked tree... She knew that place. She'd seen it in an old snapshot of herself, her sister, Jeanie, and their parents standing in the exact spot. It was one of the last pictures taken of her father before he'd disappeared eighteen years ago. The last time her family had been whole. The last moment of her childhood. Being the oldest, she'd had to grow up overnight to help her mother. She'd been in charge ever since.

She searched for the photographer's name or some kind of location tag, but found nothing to follow up on. The ad simply read, *South Central Texas.*

Thinking of her boss, Dee said, "Well, Jim, maybe you've done me a favor after all." She picked up a pen to make a note of the post-office box number and address. This was personal.

It was a slim chance, but she couldn't pass up any opportunity to put the mystery to rest. In a roundabout way, her dad's disappearance and her search for information about him had started her on the journalistic path. Years ago she'd given up ever finding out what happened to him, but her mother never had. Ellen Cates had refused to have her husband declared dead and consequently never remarried. If Dee could learn *anything* to help her mother go on with her life, she had to try.

She studied the smiling man in the picture again. In her professional opinion, the outright sexiness of his smile ought to be against the law. At least the guy didn't look as smarmy as some of the men she'd interviewed for this piece. And it wasn't as if she intended to marry him. She would answer the ad, interview him, then find out where the picture had been taken. Piece of cake.

She dialed the program director's extension. Without preamble, she said, "Okay, I'm going after the Lone Star Lover."

1

MATT TRAVIS had to slam the passenger-side door of Bill's truck twice to force it shut.

"Why don't you get that thing fixed?" he asked as he met Bill Hazard, the man who'd insisted on driving, at the front of the truck.

Bill harrumphed once. "Hell, I think of it as a battle scar. This truck ought to have been awarded a Purple Heart after being rammed by those two jail-breakin' jackrabbits." A sly look crossed his face. "Not all of us receive awards and get famous for bein' shot in the line of duty like you do. The rest of us Department of Safety employees quietly wear our scars and go about our business."

Matt pulled his Stetson a little lower over his eyes. He and Bill had had this conversation before. The man had a mind like a snapping turtle—once it clamped down on an idea, it just wouldn't let go. If he and Bill hadn't been friends since God made apple trees, things might have gotten ugly. As it was, he was used to a little Ranger bashing once in a while.

"I've told you forty times I didn't have anything to do with getting that award. The captain was lookin' for some good PR and he picked me.

You know I hate feeling like a prize bull on display, but I couldn't refuse. And if I'd known my *friends* were going to torture me over it, I'd have given it back." Searching for a way to change the subject, Matt stopped midstride and, bracing his hands on his hips, looked around the parking lot of the bar. "What do you suppose Hurly is serving tonight? I don't think I've ever seen so many cars in this lot."

Bill kept walking. "Probably somebody's birthday."

It only took two long strides for Matt to catch up. "Maybe he broke down and hired a band like we've been tellin' him."

"Maybe," Bill said, reaching for the worn handle of the wooden door. As he pulled it open, he motioned for Matt to go in first. Matt walked into the bar...and stopped dead in his tracks.

HE COULDN'T BELIEVE his eyes. The shock drove the air out of his lungs and made his ears buzz. He felt dizzy, as if someone had taken his brain and spun it like a roulette wheel. He was facing a life-size poster of himself suspended from the ceiling and surrounded by women.

It wasn't his birthday. He hadn't been promoted. He was pretty sure he wasn't dreaming. And, because he was standing inside the door of the Hole in the Wall bar, he knew he hadn't died and gone to heaven.

He blinked, but the roomful of women watching him expectantly remained solid and real.

Then, as if they'd seen a signal, they all started talking at once and moving forward.

"Matt?"

"Matthew!"

"Mr. Travis."

Matt's left hand automatically went to his hat. His granny had cuffed him and his brothers enough times when they were boys to ensure that he always remembered to remove it whenever he entered a room. His right hand moved closer to the spot where his holstered automatic usually rested at his hip. Then he remembered he'd left it in the trunk of his car. Good thing, because a few of the females staring at him looked like the greedy kind, the kind that might grab a man's gun.

Mr. Travis? Nobody called him mister. It was Officer or Ranger, or Sergeant...or Matt. Only his mother had ever called him Matthew, and then it had usually been followed by the words, "Wait till your daddy gets home!" These unfamiliar women were looking for *him?* A whole barful of them?

He aimed an incredulous "What the hell is this?" gaze at Bill and part of the puzzle snapped into place. His so-called buddy, Bill, was smiling. Always a bad sign. Bill only smiled when the bad guys were locked up, or when one of his legendary pranks had hit pay dirt. Before Matt could ask him what was so funny, the group of women broke around them like a wave on the gulf at high tide.

There were short ones, tall ones, plump ones, skinny ones, blondes, brunettes and redheads. The mix of several different varieties of perfume nearly smothered him.

Matt forgot to worry about the absence of his gun as he fought to pull his hat close to his chest. *Don't mess with my hat.*

"Whoa, whoa. What's goin' on here?" he asked.

At that moment, the bright lights of a television video camera switched on in the back of the room. Matt squinted in that direction and frowned. He could see the logo for KAUS. What the hell were they doing here?

"Hi! My name's Shirley," one of the women introduced herself.

"I'm Lisa."

"Judy."

"Sam."

Sam? Matt looked down at the eager faces surrounding him and swallowed. *It could be worse,* he realized. He could be surrounded by angry husbands. Although, at least then he would've known what to say. *I didn't do it.* Wearin' another man's boots wasn't his style.

A city-bred blonde with a microphone maneuvered through the crowd followed by a cameraman. This woman seemed to be enjoying the whole thing a little too much, in his opinion. As if his predicament was prime-time entertainment. Her smile, not to mention her legs, could have given a lesser man heart palpitations. He'd always been partial to a woman in a skirt, even if the skirt happened to be part of a business suit.

Unfortunately, when she reached Matt the smile dimmed and she stuck the mike in his face. All business.

"So, Mr. Travis, how do you feel about the—" one of her manicured hands swept the crowd of women "—overwhelming response to your ad?"

Matt decided he had to be dreaming. This was a nightmare. The television lady had used the right word—overwhelming. Why couldn't this particular dream have been about a deserted island, with the two of them stranded? His imagination began to toy with the fantasy of what he might find under that prim business suit. He cleared his throat and looked the reporter in the eye. He could handle one woman at a time—even a woman who could give Michelle Pfeiffer a run for her money in the looks department. Might as well start by answering her questions. "What ad?"

"Your ad in *Texas Men Magazine.*" She glanced around expectantly, and one of the women produced a magazine folded open. Matt took it from her and stared down at his own smiling face. The same face reproduced in the life-size poster.

Dallas oilman? Big-game hunter? Looking for a down-home Texas girl? Stunned, Matt stared at the words. This had to be a mistake. Why in the world would someone use his picture and make up such a pack of lies?

After a long pause, he raised his gaze until it

connected with the three grinning men sitting at the bar. Partners in law enforcement, and in this particular crime: Bill Hazard, Narcotics Division, Tom Wilkes and Johnny Alvarado from the State Patrol. As he watched, they raised long-necked bottles of beer in a toast.

Lone Star Lover? Matt felt his blood pressure rise. "You low-down sons of bi—"

"Mr. Travis?" the reporter cut him off. "How do you feel about—"

"Will you turn that thing off?" Matt returned the favor of interrupting. He didn't want what he was about to do to be caught on film.

"Which thing?" she retorted without missing a beat, nearly distracting him with the cheerfulness of her accompanying smile. Yes, she *was* enjoying herself 'bout half a step too much.

After awarding her a dark look instead of an answer, he gripped the magazine in one fist and stepped toward the bar. The women around him shifted back, then fell into step behind him.

He stuck the magazine under Bill's nose. "Do you mind tellin' me what the—" Some distant, public-relations part of his brain realized that the camera lights were still on, which probably meant the sound was too. "What the *heck* is this all about?"

Bill sat up a little straighter and slowly put his beer down on the bar. He waited until the microphone was close enough to be sure it would pick up his words.

"Well, son—" with a serious face he indicated

the two men on either side of him "—Johnny, Tom and I decided it's time for you to settle down and get married." His mouth kicked up on one side as he fought a smile. "We've all tried it once, so it's your turn." His knowing gaze ricocheted over the surrounding women then returned to Matt. "You should be passin' on those sterling, heroic qualities you possess to the next generation," he said solemnly. "Everybody knows that the men in your family are known for being upstanding *family* men." A murmur of agreement echoed through the crowd.

When Matt didn't rise to the bait, the reporter spoke, amusement in her low voice. "It's a good thing you wore boots today, Mr. Travis. Seems things are getting a little deep in here."

Matt glanced at her, and she looked back. She was definitely a seriously good-lookin' woman, he decided, with a smoky voice that flowed through him like the bone-deep relief of hitting smooth, seamless blacktop after driving eighty miles on gravel roads. He studied her mouth, then remembered his own rules and checked her left hand. The space on her ring finger was vacant. He took another long look at her and wondered whose name she whispered in the dark.

Now, if his misguided friends had chosen someone like her to foist on him, he wouldn't have cause to complain. She'd called him mister. That wasn't much of a start. She did seem to be onto Bill's line of bull, however, and that was promising. But before he could get used to the idea she might be on *his* side, she pushed the mike closer to catch his response.

Trapped.

He ran a hand over his face, sighed and handed the crumpled magazine back to the woman who'd volunteered it. Then he faced Bill again.

"You know what I think? I think you should apologize to all these...ladies, for wasting their time."

He could tell by the mischievous look on Bill's face that he wasn't about to surrender so easily.

"We're not wastin' their time. You're here and single. And, you better hurry up and pick one before they start to fight." Bill had the nerve to chuckle at his own humor before he turned to the crowd and raised his voice, imitating a sideshow hawker. "Ladies, I give you the *Lone Star Lover.*"

The babble of introductions rose once more, and Matt, after skewering Bill with a scowl that promised homicide, did his best to fend them off and remain a gentleman.

The gorgeous TV lady didn't help. She organized a line, strategically placed in front of his larger-than-life facsimile, and began filming the introductions. Someone brought him a bar stool but he wasn't about to participate by placing his butt in the hot seat. He rested his hat on the stool instead and watched in amazement as, under the reporter's instructions, each woman stepped up and gave her very own sales pitch. One by one they smiled at the camera, said a little bit about themselves then moved out of the way for the next candidate. It was worse than the damn "Dating Game."

"My name is Sheila. I'm from Hawthorne, Texas. I have five older brothers. I figure *Texas Men Magazine* is my best chance to find a man who isn't afraid of my family." She batted her lashes, sizing up Matt with a ten-carat sparkle in her eye. "You look like you could handle just about anything."

2

DEE CATES ALMOST laughed out loud at the expression on the Lone Star Lover's face. Interviewing him was going to be more fun than she'd expected.

God, she loved this job.

It was obvious Mr. Travis didn't know how to respond to this outpouring of feminine adoration. He, or whoever had placed the ad for him, had gotten far more than they'd bargained for. The poor guy looked totally bewildered. Spared having to make a reply about exactly what he *could* handle by the next woman stepping in front of the camera, he leveled his gaze on Dee.

A sizzle of awareness came to life inside her. He looked different than he did in his photograph, more serious, more...something. Dee Cates, the fastest composer of sound bites, couldn't quite put a label on this one. But whatever the *something* was, it broadcast the fact that there might be more to this cowboy than an empty hat and a pair of scuffed boots. And he wanted something from her, she could see it in his eyes. But what?

She took a long, lingering look at Mr. Lone Star. He'd removed his hat earlier, revealing thick, dark brown hair just long enough for a woman to run her fingers through. In person, he seemed taller, sturdier. A man who shouldered responsibilities rather than a carefree grinning cowboy standing next to a hot sports car. His picture in the magazine might have been impressive if she'd been looking for a man. She wasn't. Especially a man who had used his photo as date bait. Still, the flesh-and-blood man staring at her, frowning, made her...nervous.

Ridiculous. Being nervous and being a feature reporter were mutually exclusive. She'd interviewed men in prison on death row without a twinge. Of course, there had been bars between them but...

Dee decided not to notice. Unlike these other women, she had to remain in control. She couldn't afford the luxury of a hormone attack. She had a job to do. Besides, Mr. Lone Star had a whole roomful of willing women to stare at. He'd snared more fish than he could fry. And it was about time he started cooking for the entertainment of her viewing audience. She pulled her gaze away from his and held the microphone for the next "contestant."

"Hi, Matthew," the woman purred. "My name is Carol Ann."

This one had potential, Dee admitted, if he liked the obvious type. Carol Ann might have a chance if she'd comb some of the hair spray out of her hair and stop doing a bad Pamela Lee impression. And unless cleavage had gone out of style in the last thirty seconds or so, Carol Ann certainly had all the right equipment.

"I'm just a down-home girl—" she awarded Lone Star a hot look that could fry his bacon, then drew in a deep breath to accentuate her...assets "—lookin' for a *real* man to love."

When the *real* man in question only crossed his arms and nodded a dazed hello in response, she continued, "I know I can make you a warm and lovin' wife. I know what a husband wants."

Dee couldn't resist that opening. And suddenly, though she'd never admit it, she wanted to shuffle Carol Ann out of the picture, so to speak. She'd decided this cowboy deserved more than a partner with an IQ of 40DD. "Have you been married before then?" Dee asked innocently.

Carol Ann jumped as if she'd been awakened from a particularly satisfying dream. "Only twice," she answered, her voice losing its breathy tone and rising in pitch.

"I see. Anything else you'd like to say to the Lone Star Lover?" Dee went on.

"Yes." Carol Ann's tone went all gushy and smooth once more. She drew herself up and smiled at Matt. "If you choose me, I promise, you won't be sorry." After blowing a kiss in his direction, she sashayed away.

Raising her eyebrows in question, Dee fanned herself. "Is it getting warm in here? Or is it just me?" she asked no one in particular.

The Lone Star Lover lowered his hands to rest on his hips and leveled a warning gaze at her. He looked as though he wanted to give her a spanking. Oops! Laughing at her own thoughts, she gestured for the next woman to step forward.

Finally, after ten or so auditions, Matthew "Lone Star Lover" Travis plucked the microphone out of Dee's hand, transferred it to the cameraman and pulled her aside.

"Look, Miss—"

"Cates," she filled in and offered her hand. "Dee Cates from KAUS."

Matt looked at her hand for a moment before giving it a brief, firm shake. "Miss Cates. May I ask what kind of story you intend to do about this—" he glanced up at the group of waiting women "—this fi-ass-co?"

Dee had a hard time reining in her genuine amusement at his way with words. "Certainly you *may*. I'm doing a story on dating in the nineties. This will be great footage for the segment on personal ads." He seemed concerned at the prospect, and she couldn't resist teasing him just a bit. "Don't tell me after putting your picture in a regional magazine that you're afraid of a little more publicity."

MATT KNEW he was frowning, and in the past his frown had been enough to make some criminals think twice. But Dee Cates didn't seem at all intimidated by him.

"That's just it. I didn't put my picture in the magazine." He pointed to the three culprits, his so-called friends, still ensconced at the bar. "They did."

"Really?" Her smile remained, and she looked unconvinced.

Matt put a hand over his heart. "I swear. I had nothing to do with this whole thing."

Her gaze dropped to the hand he'd raised and her smile dimmed by a few watts. He could almost hear her mind working. "Well, I'll tell you what. I got some great stuff tonight." She brought her gaze back to his. "If you'll give me an interview telling your side of the story, we can add the voice-over to the footage we have and use it for an anecdote."

"A what?"

"You know, a funny sort of sidebar to the story."

Matt didn't like that idea worth a damn. He'd had enough of being the center of attention. "I see. The joke is on me, again. For the benefit of the television audience."

"Not really. It would give you a chance to tell the truth about the ad. And…" Her eyes sparkled with humor, and for the first time Matt noticed the color—blue. Texas-sky blue. The kind of eyes that could coax the common sense right out of a man. "It might be a way to turn the joke around on your friends."

Matt had to force his mind back to the business at hand. Getting back at Bill, Johnny and Tom was an idea worth considering, he decided. And even if he couldn't roast 'em, he could at least convince everyone the ad wasn't real. Maybe salvage his reputation. Then he noticed that several of the women had stepped closer and were listening to the conversation. His instinct for self-preservation kicked in. What would these women do when they found out they'd come all this distance for nothing? He wasn't going to choose any of them. And he definitely wasn't going to stick around and explain why.

He managed what he hoped was a friendly, co-operative smile and aimed it at Miss Cates. "I tell *you* what. I'll give you an interview if you'll drive me back to my car. I left it in town."

She hesitated for a moment, and he continued, "No cameraman. Just you and me. And," he added, "we leave right now."

Miss Cates didn't hesitate this time. Nodding, she turned on a dime and went to talk to her cameraman. Matt made his way to the bar and pulled out his wallet. After a short conversation with the bartender, he met Dee at the door.

"Are you ready?" she asked. She had some keys and her briefcase.

"Just a second," Matt answered.

"Ladies!" The bartender said loudly. "The Lone Star Lover would like to buy you a beer."

Matt stepped forward and raised a hand to claim their attention. "I appreciate the opportunity to meet you all." He smiled in what he hoped was a politically correct way and added, "If you'll leave your names and numbers and any personal messages you might like to add with my friends at the bar—" he gestured to the three cohorts in crime "—I'll be in touch."

The noise level in the room rose dramatically as the women headed for the bar. Matt laughed in satisfaction when he saw the comical looks of Bill, Tom, and Johnny. Now *they* were surrounded by females. He offered them a sarcastic salute before taking Miss Cates's arm and propelling both of them out the door.

3

DEE LEANED across the console of the station's car and unlocked the passenger door. As the tall cowboy folded himself into the seat next to her, she wondered if she'd done the right thing. Leaving a bar with a strange man wasn't the most dangerous thing she'd done in the pursuit of a story. But normally she had a plan and a backup in case the first one failed. Right now, she was winging it.

Then, as if he sensed her uneasiness, he looked at her and grinned. "Miz Cates," he drawled. "I think you may have just saved my life."

The effect was dazzling, even in the dim light of the parking lot. A bright sizzle of pleasure ran through her. Dee wondered if he knew the potency of his boyish grin. If just once he'd smiled that way in the bar, the mob scene would have become a free-for-all, like dropping one extra-large chocolate truffle in a roomful of half-starved women.

And then she envisioned herself in the crowd, fighting for her own satisfying bite. The idea was appalling. This had gone far enough. She had to get her fantasies under control. She was known for keeping her professional life...well, *profes-*

sional. Wouldn't her boss love it...Dee Cates lassoed by a cowboy.

In your dreams, Lone Star, she thought, then busied herself starting the car while changing the subject. "Well, at this point, I feel compelled to say that I hope you are who you said you are and not some serial killer."

The door to the bar swung open as Dee shifted and headed across the gravel parking lot to the road.

"Who did I say I was?" the cowboy asked as he looked behind them toward the women spilling out of the Hole in the Wall, with Carol Ann in the lead.

"An oilman?" Dee said, suddenly realizing how little that description covered.

The cowboy turned back to her as they picked up speed southbound toward San Antonio. "Oilmen are as common as mesquite. I can do better than that." He removed his hat and stuck out his hand. "Sergeant Matt Travis, Texas Ranger."

Dee put her hand in his briefly. It was the second time she'd touched him, but this time she cautioned herself to ignore the effect. He was grinning again and she felt overpowered by the tangible warmth of it. *Control,* her mind whispered like a mantra. She pulled her hand away and concentrated on the road. *A Texas Ranger.* That was more than she'd hoped for. Now if she could only figure out how to get him to help her without becoming a mating candidate.

"So, you really didn't place the ad?"

"No, ma'am." His grin faded slightly. "I guess you could say I have friends in low places."

Ma'am. That brought her up short. *Ma'am* was something men called their high-school teachers, or little old ladies, or, their mothers. She should have been comforted by the implied distance, but for some reason, it irritated her coming from him. A part of her wanted him to think of her as a woman—as much of a woman as any of those in the bar earlier. Before she could decipher the source of that wayward thought, she remembered she was supposed to be working.

"Oh, wait a second." Dee fumbled around, searching for her briefcase. She swung it into the front and pushed it toward Matt. "Would you get my tape recorder out of there, please?"

He glanced down at the briefcase then back to her. "There's nothin' in there that's going to bite me, is there?"

She gave him a quelling look, the sound of his "ma'am" echoing in the part of her brain assigned to paybacks. "Surely a Texas Ranger isn't afraid of a briefcase?"

"Well, no, not the briefcase. Part of my business is gettin' into risky situations. But when I was a kid, my granny taught me always to be careful about where I put my hands and my bare feet. Since then, I've learned some other things to be careful with."

His words brought to mind parts of his anatomy that she didn't want to discuss—unless it had to do with his dating habits. *Let's not go there,* she coaxed silently. Because she wasn't sure she could direct where they'd end up.

Dee decided to play dumb, which came in handy sometimes, even though it irritated her that the ruse worked so well. She was blond, after all. "Well, I promise, there's nothing dangerous in there."

Without further argument, he dug into the case and found her tape recorder. With practiced moves she pushed the record button and set the machine on the dash in front of him. *When in doubt, get back to business.* "You promised me an interview."

"Yeah, right." He closed the briefcase before placing it on the back seat. Then he picked up the recorder, studied it briefly and returned it to the dash. "I understand. Anything I say can and will be used against me. So, what do you want to know?"

What did she want to know? For her job, she needed to ask questions about the ad and his dating habits. But what she wanted, no, *needed* to know had to do with Matt's picture in the magazine. The picture that might shed some light on her father's whereabouts. Too soon to ask that.

"Let's start at the beginning. When did you find out about the ad?"

Matt frowned. "When I walked through that door tonight."

"You're telling me you had no idea what was going on?"

"That's what I said. I should have guessed

something was up when Bill insisted on me driving over here with him to meet Johnny and Tom. He's had a bout with some kind of Asian flu and was taking medication. He said his wife had been after him about working late hours and driving alone." Matt made a sound of disgust and looked out the window. "I should have known that story was a load of—" He caught himself and went on. "He's gone alone on narcotics stakeouts for days at a time. I just figured he was trying to please Rayanne, uh, his wife."

"So, for the record, you were set up. Is that it?"

"Yep."

Succinct and to the point, but she needed more than that for her article. "Are you married?"

"No." Another one-word answer that sounded final. "They never would've pulled this if I was married. And if they had, I'd hope my wife would shoot 'em for it."

She couldn't let him off that easily. Besides, she wanted to know more. "Have you ever been married?"

"No, again. I got close once or twice, when I was young and foolish. Since then I've seen too many divorces. Two out of three of my buddies you met tonight are happily divorced. I want to be sure before I take the final step."

"So why are you upset with your friends? It seems like they were trying to help you find the right woman. From the turnout, I figure you'd have enough fish—I mean, dates, for the next year or so."

His frown faded, and his mouth slid into a slow smile. "Well, now, I like women. And I don't mind being wanted." Several of Dee's heartbeats went by before he continued. "But those women in the bar... They wanted something from me—money, protection, a roll in the hay—not *me*."

Before she could agree or feel guilty that she wanted something from him as well, he maneuvered the question back into her lap. "Have you found the one *you* want?"

The intimate tone of his voice bordered on erotic, although the words were innocent enough. The majority of Dee's inner defenses went on red alert. This man might look like a cowboy, but he'd taken control of the conversation as smoothly as a seasoned interviewer. And he'd reached past her normally impervious businesslike facade to her personal life. If he ever found out how his smile, his touch had set her nerves on end, she'd really be in the soup. She was glad she had to keep her eyes on the road. "Are you asking if I'm married?" she asked, stalling. When in doubt, repeat the question.

"Married or...whatever."

"No, I'm not married." She could almost hear her boss's voice adding, *yet*. "And I don't have a...whatever."

The grin returned. She could see it peripherally by the glow of the dash lights. Her mouth curled in answer but she stopped before she actually smiled. She didn't need to encourage him. And she hoped never to be in the position of being interrogated by him. She'd probably spill all her secrets and enjoy doing it. *Just move a little to the left and I'll tell you everything…*

She shook her head slightly to clear the image of having this cowboy's hands on her. "Let's get back to the ad. So, you're not an oilman… How about the big-game hunting and the exotic animals and the quarter horses? Any of that true?"

Matt Travis made an impolite sound that started with sh— and ended in a sort of cough. "The only big game I hunt travels on two legs and usually has a criminal record. And as for exotic animals, if you consider an abandoned, half-starved mule I found in the hills and an armadillo I hit with my car one night exotic, then, there you have it. I plead guilty as charged."

As a woman, Dee could testify to the potency of his teasing charm. Guilty as charged. One thing was clear, Ranger Matt Travis didn't need to place any ads. All he needed was twenty minutes alone with a woman—any woman—and she'd want to know him for better, or worse. Dee couldn't afford the time to be distracted by Mr. Sexy Texas Ranger. She needed to find out about the photograph.

"What about the car in the picture? That's an expensive piece of German engineering. Does it belong to you?"

He thought about his answer for a moment as if he didn't know exactly which car she meant. "You mean the Porsche?" he said finally.

"Yes, the one by the lake."

"About three months ago... We'd just confiscated that car along with ten kilos of cocaine and two hundred and twenty thousand dollars." He crossed his arms and frowned. "That's why I was smiling. I'd been working with the narcotics and customs folks for months trying to catch the guy." Matt turned to look at her in dawning recognition. "Bill took that picture."

Guiding the conversation had been easier than she'd thought. Now for the sixty-four-thousand-dollar question. "Do you remember exactly where that photo was taken?"

Matt sat there for a moment, silent. Finally, she was forced to take her eyes off the road and glance at him.

"I remember," he said. "But before I answer, do you mind telling me what that has to do with dating in the nineties?"

Uh-oh. She'd relaxed too soon. Now he was suspicious. Perfectly natural for a Ranger, she supposed. "I just wondered," she said in an offhand manner, hoping he'd let it go. But then she realized she was too close to keep circling the question without knowing the answer. She reached up and switched off the tape recorder. Time for the truth.

"Do you remember saying that all those women in the bar wanted something from you?"

He nodded.

"Well, I want something from you too."

THE INSISTENT *beep, beep, beep* from a pager cut through the silence after Dee's statement. Annoyed by the interruption, Matt pulled the pager from his belt, shut off the beeper, then tipped it to pick up the lights from the car behind them. He didn't recognize the number, but Rangers were technically always on duty. He had to return the call.

"There's a portable phone in my briefcase," Dee suggested.

Matt reached for the briefcase again, extracted the phone and dialed.

"Hole in the Wall," a voice said over the sound of a jukebox in the background.

Matt recognized Johnny's voice. He hoped the three pranksters would have to call for backup.

"What do you want now?" Matt asked abruptly. He'd rather talk to Dee than be hassled by his so-called friends. She'd just made one helluva provocative statement. He intended to hear the punch line.

"Hey, Mat-thew," Johnny said. "Where'd you run off to?"

"Why? Do you need help with cleavage control?"

"Ha. Ha. Ha. No. I think we can manage, even without a Ranger. But listen, we went to a lot of trouble to fix you up, then you turn tail out of here like a young buck at his first social." Johnny made a clucking sound into the phone. "I've seen you face down armed felons. I never would have thought you'd get so chicken-livered around a bunch of females."

Matt laughed. "If there wasn't a lady present, I'd tell you exactly what I think of you boys fixing me up. Let's just leave it at this. How about *not* doing me any favors from now on?"

Matt heard a voice say something in the background but it was muddled by the music. Then Johnny spoke again. "Oh, I almost forgot. We did you one last favor…"

"What now?" Matt closed his eyes and waited for the ax to fall.

"We gave all these eligible ladies your home phone number," he answered. "And we loaned them a roll of quarters." Matt could tell his friend was grinning.

More laughter erupted in the background. Then a voice yelled, "Yeah, and we had one of them write it on the bathroom wall. For a good time, call…"

"Y-you what?" Matt stuttered.

Johnny continued. "Just so you wouldn't lose touch and miss out on finding your Ms. Right. Your answering machine should run out of tape in the next fifteen minutes or so. Have a nice day," Johnny said and hung up the phone.

Matt switched the power off and pinched the bridge of his nose.

"Is everything all right?" Dee asked.

"Oh yeah. Just great," Matt answered as he shoved the phone back into her briefcase. "You may have a real story here. You can use the film you took of me on the ten o'clock news. 'Texas Ranger goes beserk and hunts down three fellow officers,'" he announced in an official-sounding voice. There was a certain satisfaction just thinking about it, Matt decided.

The silence that followed his pronouncement made him study Dee. She looked unsure, and he realized she might actually believe him. He took the opportunity to devil her a little bit. "They gave my home phone number to all those women," he said in an injured tone. "Don't you think that's just cause for homicide?"

"Well, I…"

"Oh, and you were going to tell me you wanted something from me, too. What exactly would that be?"

"I…um… We just passed the first exit to San Antonio. Where did you say you left your car?"

Matt couldn't hide his grin. If Miss Dee Cates had been a dancer, she'd be tapping as fast as she could right about now. "Now, Mz. Cates, you sound nervous. You're not afraid of being alone in a car on the east side of nowhere with me? Are you? I'm not armed or dangerous."

She glanced at him again, and the corner of her mouth kicked up. She knew he was teasing her. He watched the tenseness drain out of her hands gripping the wheel.

"I'm as harmless as an old toothless dog lyin' in a patch of summer shade," he offered.

"Coming from a man who usually carries a gun and is armed with a lethal smile that could melt an iceberg, I seriously doubt that."

"Now, that melting part. That's what I'd like to

talk about. We were discussing my love life. What is it you wanted to ask me?"

She went serious on him again. "Don't get your hopes up. I wasn't going to ask for a demonstration. First, give me directions to your car so I know where I'm going."

Matt shifted his attention to the landscape. They were on the outskirts of San Antonio. "There's a little restaurant off exit 78. I left it in the parking lot. I'll tell you when to turn."

He shifted slightly toward her in the seat and waited for her to say what she wanted to say. But even his ever-present optimism wasn't predicting that she might be interested in him. Instead, she probably had some silly thing she wanted him to do for her TV audience.

It seemed to take a long time for her to decide what to ask. They were approaching the exit which would bring them to his car when she finally decided to spit it out.

"I want you to tell me how to find the lake where your friend took that picture." She glanced at him sideways. "The picture in the magazine."

Now if this didn't frost the cake. What in the world would make a woman like her drive all this way to see a dam and a lake in the middle of nowhere? Was she beautiful *and* crazy? He decided to try teasing the truth out of her.

"Why? You plannin' to do some fishin'?"

4

FISHING? Here she was being serious and this, this *cowboy* was still playing games. As tempting as it might be to relax, Dee couldn't do it. She'd learned long ago that being in control meant safety. Even if that safety sometimes kept people at a distance.

"Turn left at the next exit," he said, without missing a beat.

Dee hit the brakes and turned. When they reached the parking lot of the Los Amigos Tex-Mex Restaurant, she pulled into a spot next to a nondescript, gold-colored sedan, shifted the car into park then turned to face him with her best no-nonsense expression.

"Don't you ever get serious?" she asked, half-way up the road of exasperation. She couldn't read the look on his face with any accuracy, so she answered the question. "No, I'm not planning on fishing—in that lake or any other. I just need to know where it is."

He met her gaze steadily. Two cars navigated through the parking lot, giving Dee time to regret her contrariness before he spoke. "North of here. Up near the dam at Canyon Lake."

"Thank you," she said, feeling as if she'd just wrestled a steer to the ground.

"And, yes, I do get serious. Seriousness is part of being a Texas Ranger. But I try not to let it take over my off-time." The decidedly unserious gleam returned to his eyes. "So, what's so important about that lake?" he asked. "If you *were* a fisher— Uh, a fisher-person, I'd say you'd find more bass over at Calaveras. Braunig Lake is closer. Did some fool tell you that people go out there on dates?"

"No. My interest has nothing to do with my story on dating. It's personal." She tried to leave it at that because he'd really think she was crazy if she told him an eighteen-year-old picture had been taken at the same lake. At least she thought it was the same one. And that she believed going there would somehow lead her to her father. "What's the best way to get there?" she asked as if the answer didn't matter much.

"It's a good ways from here. You're not thinking about going out there now, are you?"

"Do you *always* answer a question with a question?"

"Only when there's something I want to know." He crossed his arms, waiting. "I'm a curious man." He looked more stubborn than curious. Stubborn enough to stay until she provided some answers. Well, she'd wanted him to get serious...

Dee sighed and gave up. He obviously wasn't going to get out of her car until she satisfied his curiosity. "Yes, I thought I might ride by there. To see if I remembered it right. I think I was there once before, a long time ago."

Finally, he opened the car door. "We'll take my car," he said and got out.

"Hey—" Dee was forced to unbuckle her seat belt and get out as well. She propped her arms on the top of the car and faced him as he settled his Stetson. "I'm perfectly capable of driving myself, if you'll just give me directions."

"Any man who sends you off alone—at night—on a long road to nothin' isn't a gentleman." He shifted his hands to his hips. "And he certainly isn't a Ranger. I happen to be both, or so my mama likes to believe. If you insist on sightseein' by moonlight, then I'm going to be your tour guide. Call it public relations." He smiled before walking to the back of his car and opening the trunk. Dee watched as he unzipped a leather gym bag, took out his gun belt and fastened it around his waist. "You can tell me why while I'm drivin'."

So much for control. Dee couldn't see any way around taking a ride with Ranger Matt Travis. Part of her didn't mind at all. At least he knew the area. And a tall man with a gun might come in handy on a lonely stretch of road at night. She didn't want to think about what else Ranger Matt Travis might be handy at in the dark. Determined to keep things strictly business, she grabbed her purse and briefcase before locking the station's car. He held the door open for her as she slid into his car. By the time he closed it, she'd decided to tell him the truth. She wanted his help, she just wasn't sure he'd take her seriously.

He drove as if he spent half his life on the road, not slow but not breakneck. Before Dee got settled properly, they were leaving San Antonio behind and heading north under the clear star-filled, waxing-moon sky, the silence punctuated occasionally by a low level of police chatter on the radio.

A few miles out of town, Matt draped one hand over the wheel and rested the other on his thigh. He still looked relaxed, but his expression had changed. She'd wanted serious, that's what she received. As if putting on his gun and getting in his car had taken every bit of the teasing out of him. "Now, you want to tell me what this is all about?" he asked.

"Well..."

He gave her that same steady, I-can-wait-all-night kind of look that wrestled with her restraint and made Dee feel like saying, *All right, already!* Then he shifted his gaze back to the road.

"We lived in Oklahoma at the time," she said at last. "My dad collected Indian artifacts from most of the western states. We came through this area on a family vacation when I was twelve years old, the summer of 1980." She stopped staring at his profile and looked out at the lights from the businesses they were passing. "I've gone over that trip a thousand times in my mind, but I only have a few memories. My mother has a picture, though, and I think it was taken on the same lake I've been asking you about."

There, she'd said it. She waited for him to laugh and call her a sentimental fool. He did neither.

"Why is that trip so important? Or do you visit every place your family traveled?"

Nothing like getting straight to the point. She might as well follow suit. "I've visited a few, but that particular trip was the last one we ever took as a family. Just after that photo was taken, my father disappeared."

"Disappeared?"

"He left us at the motel one afternoon and didn't come back."

"Did your mother file a report with the Sheriff's department?"

"Yes, of course. And they located our car on the side of the road about ten miles from the lake with a flat tire, but they never found my dad."

He mulled over the information for a moment, then asked, "What do you hope to find out there now?"

This was the hard part. How could she tell him she was running on pure instinct? Sentimental instinct at that. An embarrassing admission from a woman who depended on fact not fiction. She was the oldest daughter. When her father disappeared, she'd been forced to grow up in the space of a few months. Somehow she'd always thought it was her job to find out the truth for her mother.

"Nothing, I guess. Your picture reminded me of that time, and I had to at least see the place again with my own eyes. One day we were like a hundred other families visiting the lake, and the next day, my father was gone."

Dee vividly remembered the long silent trip home, the even longer nights over the rest of that summer when she would listen as her mother cried herself to sleep. Every year after seemed to be shaped and shadowed by her father's absence in their lives: graduation from high school, then college, Dee's first job, her sister's marriage and the births of her children. All of those events seemed partially empty because of one summer day when her father had gone out alone.

A few more moments of silence passed as they drove. They left the main highway and took a two-lane road. The night-shadowed area seemed flat at first, then as the road twisted they entered the low rolling, tree-covered hills. Soon, the headlights illuminated signs up ahead for Canyon Lake Dam. Matt turned left after a sign that said Slow Down and See Our Dam. Speed Up and See Our Dam Judge.

They drove along the grassy slanted expanse of a man-made hill before the road took a sharp turn upward. The sign said the park was closed, but it was easy enough to maneuver around the gate. After driving up a long embankment, Canyon Lake glinted under a fat, nearly full moon.

As they reached level road, Matt slowed further and turned off into a roadside park. He stopped the car, unfastened his seat belt, got out, then walked around to open Dee's door.

"This is it," he announced.

Matt offered his hand to help her out of the car. She surprised him by taking it. He didn't know what to expect next from this woman. One minute she was all business, a reporter interrogating him about his personal life, the next she seemed unsure, allowing him to help with her personal problems. He didn't want to do anything to disrupt that delicate balance. So, instead of staring at her legs as she stepped out of the car, he concentrated on the smoothness of her hand. Manners required him to let it go sooner than he wanted.

She gave him a brief smile before turning and walking away, back toward the dam.

"Do you recognize anything?" he asked.

Without pulling her gaze from the moonlit scenery, she answered, "I should have brought the picture...but yes, I'm fairly certain this is the place. I remember my sister and I had gone swimming." She shifted her attention to the edge of the lake and squinted into the darkness. "I remember a lot of rocks on the shore."

"What about your mother? Does she remember anything significant about the lake?"

Dee's gaze lowered for a moment. "My mother stopped talking about my dad years ago. She doesn't seem strong enough to go through it all again."

No help there. Matt tried to think of ways to jog an eighteen-year-old memory. He raised a hand toward the distant shoreline. "There's a marina on the other side of those trees. I'd have to look up the county records to see how long it's been there."

"Could we go down to the water?"

"Sure."

Matt moved up beside her just as she stepped off the blacktop onto the rocky ground and stumbled. The trail was a little steep and lit only by moonlight. He had to catch her arm above the elbow to keep her upright.

"Well, you're right about the rocks," he said, keeping her steady. He liked the fact that she gripped his arm, but he tried not to enjoy it too much. He looked down. "Those shoes aren't gonna cut it. You need some nice sensible boots to walk out here."

"That's what I remember. When we went swimming the rocks hurt our feet." She took another careful step but didn't let go of his arm. "Going barefoot would be worse."

She didn't ask and he didn't offer—he simply moved forward and kept her upright. Hell, he would have carried her, but putting his arms around her in the dark might be misinterpreted. Besides, he liked the feel of her holding on to him. Being a gentleman had its perks.

By the time they reached the shore, he was chuckling over her unsteady steps. When he caught her smiling in response, Matt was reluctant to let her go. He stayed close, just in case.

A slight breeze ruffled the surface of the lake, and the bright moonlight reflected a silver trail to their feet. The cooler air smelled heavy, as though it carried the fresh water from the lake.

DEE DREW IN a deep breath, searching for memories of a sunny day eighteen years before. She couldn't come up with much. The place seemed the same, but now, in the dark so many years later, she'd lost the connecting thread. Her father's disappearance shortly after their visit had clouded the happy memories.

At that moment, she felt more conscious of the present than the past. Here she was standing in the dark with a man she barely knew, a man who, with one sexy grin, could make her heart pound like a schoolgirl's. Yet even though he made her tremble inside, she felt...safe. Without questions or comment he'd held out his arm to her and helped her limp out over the rocks. He'd let her decide how much assistance she needed. By the time they'd reached even ground, it seemed so natural to have his arm around her, she'd been reluctant to let him go. She glanced up at him in the moonlight. He met her gaze with a serious expression.

"If you're gonna go swimmin', you'll have to break the law," he said in a deadpan tone.

"Break the law?"

His mouth shifted as he subdued a smile. "Well, you don't swim in your clothes, do you?"

"Not usually," she answered, giving in to the urge to one-up him. She watched his eyes as he chose his reply.

"If it helps you to decide, I have to inform you I don't swim with my badge on."

"Does that mean you wouldn't be able to arrest me? Or that we'd both be breaking the law?"

As soon as the words were out of her mouth, the fantasy side of Dee's brain painted a Technicolor picture—complete with touch and taste—of the two of them, swimming in the moon-struck water…naked. She felt her skin heat from knees to neck. As warmth moved into her cheeks, she came to her senses, glad they were standing in the dark.

He didn't answer right away. The same darkness that prevented his seeing her blush made it difficult to gauge his reaction. Suddenly, he grinned and Dee had the feeling he'd read her thoughts. "Let's just say I've been known to be a little reckless. With that in mind, the answer is we'd both be in trouble."

She had to look away from the playfulness of his smile. If he'd offered her his hand, she might have done something foolish, like kick off her shoes and wade in. She changed the subject instead.

"Well…I'm not sure what I expected, but there doesn't seem to be much out here now to help solve the mystery."

"That's not exactly true," Matt said. "I'm here, and solving mysteries is part of my job."

He'd surprised her. Originally, she'd wanted to ask for his help, but now the idea seemed far-fetched. "I couldn't ask you to waste your time on something that happened eighteen years ago. I'm sure you have more important things to do."

Matt brought one hand up and braced it on his gun belt. "This is what we call a 'cold' case. And sometimes they're the most interesting. Tell you what. When I get home, I figure I'm gonna have to shoot my answering machine to put it out of its misery. So, I'll make you a deal."

"What kind of deal?"

"Were you planning to stay somewhere in this area to do your story?"

"You're answering a question with a question again," she reminded him. "And yes, I planned to stay in San Antonio overnight. I could take a couple of vacation days if you think you could help."

"Good. Here's the deal, then. I can't guarantee anything, but I'm willing to check around. You pretend to be my Mz. Right for a little while to get my buddies off my back, and I'll see what I can find out about your father's case."

Dee wasn't sure it was wise to be standing in the dark making any kind of deals with a man who made her think of shucking her clothes and taking a midnight swim, but she did want his help. "And what are the duties of a Mz. Right?" she asked carefully, imitating his drawl.

He smiled, making Dee's knees wobble slightly. And her unsteadiness had nothing to do with the fact that she was standing on rocks.

"Don't worry. My mama expected her sons to be gentlemen, and my granny made sure she wasn't disappointed. If I tell my buddies we hit it off, then they'll quit giving out my phone number to prospective brides. All you have to do is be seen in my company a few times. I promise not to wrestle with you."

The idea of wrestling with Matt Travis didn't seem so scary at the moment.

"Okay, Mr. Lone Star, you've got a deal."

5

"YOU'RE TAKING a what?" Jim had said in disbelief early the next morning when she'd called in.

"You heard me right. I'm taking a few days' vacation." She'd hoped to leave her message on his voice mail to circumvent his inevitable questions. Luck had failed her, however, and she'd had to endure not only a landslide of questions but his trademark ribbing as well.

"Are you sick? You never take vacations," he'd said. "You have more vacation days stacked up than Cal Ripkin, Jr."

Dee couldn't argue that point. It was true. She loved her job. She'd much rather be chasing an interview or editing a segment than lying around on some foreign beach drinking piña coladas and speaking inadequate Spanish.

Her boss thought that was weird. He was entitled to his opinion. She'd placated him by sending the footage she'd gotten at the Lone Star Lover's debut party back to Austin with Jason the cameraman, and by promising to see Jim bright and early Monday morning to get the piece ready to air the following week. Now she was on her own.

Well, not exactly. She had Matt Travis, aka the

Lone Star Lover. It remained to be seen whether that would be a blessing or a curse. Initially, she'd decided that the flamboyant ad bore little resemblance to the straightforward, low-key Ranger. But after standing with him alone in the dark…she'd reconsidered.

He certainly could be charming, especially when you least expected it. A dangerous man. Smart *and* sexy. He'd managed to talk her into pretending to be his…date. She'd have to stay on her toes to keep things professional. Or, better yet, stepping on his toes occasionally might do the trick.

Last night, just for a moment, she'd wanted to move into his arms, to challenge his reckless suggestion that they go for a swim. On second thought perhaps she *should* invest in a pair of boots, to keep her from getting in too deep.

She glanced at her watch as she locked the door to her hotel room. She had two hours before she had to meet him downtown for lunch. Time enough to visit the library and do some background checking. To get down to business again.

She planned to search the microfilm files for old newspapers published around the time her father disappeared. She also intended to find out everything she could about Ranger Matthew Travis.

MATT HUNG UP the phone and reached for his hat. He'd stopped by the courthouse to check the old county records, then spent an hour in a meeting reinterviewing a witness to a felony for the Bexar

County Sheriff's Office. Ten phone calls later, he had set the investigative process on Dee's father in motion. Now he intended to have lunch with one seriously good-looking woman—his temporary Mz. Right, Dee Cates.

He didn't have much to tell her. Cold cases, even the ones he took a personal interest in, always started slow. Finding old records and possible witnesses was like trying to travel back in time. Even a Texas Ranger wouldn't claim that particular talent. They had to rely on good old-fashioned trackin', backward and forward.

And he wanted to find something out for Dee. For a variety of reasons. Gratitude for coming to his rescue had a lot to do with it. He also wanted to keep her in the area for as long as he could. He might talk her into a moonlight swim yet. He remembered her arm hooked around his the night before as she walked down the rocky path to the lake. She'd allowed him to help her and she'd smiled in the dark. It was a start. She would've been a little more reluctant if she'd known how that simple touch had stirred up all kinds of less innocent reactions under his skin.

It had been a while since he'd been affected so strongly by a woman. And even longer since a city-bred, career-type woman like Dee had gotten under his skin. She definitely wasn't his usual style. But he wasn't quite ready to entertain the notion of letting her go just yet.

First he had to dig through the fallout from his newfound notoriety. When he'd come into his office that morning, his desk had been littered with phone messages. He hadn't even counted the ones that had been recorded on his answering machine at home. He'd simply pulled the tape, tossed it, then unplugged the beleaguered machine. No use killing the messenger.

Unfortunately, that hadn't stopped people from calling, and sometime after midnight he'd finally unplugged the phone itself. It was probably better to ignore his friends as best he could and let them wonder what he was up to.

The peace and quiet didn't last long, however. He bumped into Bill Hazard and two other DOS officers on the way to the parking lot.

"Well, if it isn't the Lone Star Lover," Bill said, grinning. "How'd it go with the TV lady? Are you gonna be on the tube tonight, a woman on each arm?"

The two officers with Bill chuckled. Obviously, word of the the fiasco at Hurly's had spread.

"I don't believe I'm speaking to you," Matt replied, forming his best frown. When Bill kept on grinnin', Matt decided it was time to bait the hook. "Of all the harebrained stunts…" He shook his head in fake disgust. "If not for meeting Dee, I might be ready to shoot you and Jimmy right about now."

"Dee?" Bill scratched his head. "Which one was that?"

"The one I left with, Miss Dee Cates, from the television station."

"You mean, out of all those women last night, you picked the TV lady?"

"Why not? I'd say she's, without a doubt, the pick of the litter." A statement he didn't need to lie about.

Bill looked scandalized. "Yeah, but that one...that Carol Ann, she was prime cut."

"A little too showy for me. Now, Bill, I thought you'd be happy I'd found my Mz. Right. Isn't that what you wanted?"

"Your Mz. Right? Are you telling me you and the TV lady—"

"Definitely a keeper," Matt concluded, reaching out to shake Bill's hand. "And that's why I'm not gonna shoot you. I'm going to thank you."

"Thank me?"

Before Bill could react properly, Matt nodded. "As a matter of fact, I'm having lunch with her." He glanced at his watch. "Don't want to be late. See you boys later."

As Matt walked toward his car, he could feel the three men's gaze like a prod between his shoulder blades. Let 'em mull that one over for a while.

"I HAD NO IDEA you were such a hero." Dee smiled at him as the hostess took them to a table in the back. The restaurant was low-key, but upscale Tex-Mex.

"Me?" Matt asked as he pulled out Dee's chair for her to sit.

"Yes, you. I read all about it in the *San Antonio*

Star. 'Texas Ranger Matthew Travis receives the Medal of Valor,'" she recited.

He shifted in his chair and placed his hat on the table near the wall before speaking. "Yeah, well, that was just one of those things about being in the right place at the right time."

"Doesn't sound like the right place to me. You were shot."

"We got the job done." His expression warned her that he'd said all he intended to say about the subject.

Dee was amazed at his offhand manner. He acted as if it was perfectly normal to face down a man with a gun. But then again, he was a Ranger.

"And the little girl wasn't hurt," she added.

The uncompromising set of his mouth softened. "No, she came out of it fine."

The waitress stopped to take their drink orders, giving Dee the opportunity to watch him change personae once more. The serious professional kicked back into cowboy mode for the benefit of the college-age server. His killer grin returned, and the waitress seemed reluctant to leave.

Dee had been a reporter too long to be sidetracked by an interruption. She'd read the facts about the case in the newspaper, but wanted to hear what happened from Matt, to see it through his eyes. When they were alone once more, she continued. "Tell me about the kidnapping."

In measured movements he picked up his water glass, took a swallow then set it down. Loosely clasping his hands in front of him, he met her gaze.

"First tell me why you want to know. Is this something you want to put on TV about the Lone Star Lover?"

He didn't trust her. She couldn't blame him for that. But the disparity between Matt Travis, the Lone Star Lover, and Matt Travis, Texas Ranger, was too great to be useful in her story. Her dating-in-the-nineties piece was filled with sexy details, not grim reality.

"It's not for the story. I would like to know."

He gazed at her for another long moment before beginning. "He took her at night," he said and looked away. "Ray Abrams, the kidnapper, had worked for the little girl's father about six months before the foreman of the ranch fired him. Since Ray knew the father owned the biggest insurance company in the area, and he'd been around long enough to know the house, he went in and snatched the man's five-year-old daughter right out of her bed. Then he asked for a million dollars' ransom and a car.

"He'd holed up in an old hunting cabin out in the scrub and kept in touch with the family by cellular phone."

"The girl's parents must have gone crazy."

"We did what we could to reassure them. Abrams had no record as a child molester, but that didn't mean he wouldn't hurt her if he was cornered. Or, that he wouldn't kill her out of spite if his plan failed.

"The hardest part was keeping her father from charging the place with a gun. I had to give the man my word I would get his daughter out of there."

"How could you be sure that you'd be able to keep a promise like that?"

"I intended to keep it or die tryin'."

The idea of Matt putting himself in that kind of danger sent a shiver over her skin. "So you went into the house?"

"No, not inside. We didn't have a chance in Hades of getting in before he hurt her. We gave him what he wanted. Sort of.

"We got a brand-new Cadillac off the lot of a local dealer and had the windows tinted like he asked. We even put the money he'd demanded in the trunk. When it came time to deliver it though, we added a little something extra."

"You?"

"Yeah. Me and another DOS officer. I had given my word and I had no family depending on me. Sammy Hart volunteered to go with me. He drove the car and I hid behind the seat."

Matt smiled faintly. "Let me tell you, it gives new meaning to the phrase *back-seat driving.* Sammy talked to me all the way until we pulled up in front of the house. Then Wilks used the girl as a shield and forced Sammy to walk away from the car. I couldn't see a damn thing, but when he opened the back door and shoved her in, I jumped up.

"Things happened real fast after that. I remember pulling the girl behind me before he got the first shot off. I fired back, but it was Sammy who took him down."

"You could have been killed."

He shrugged in casual agreement. "Yeah, I suppose things were a little precarious there for a few minutes. The Memorial Cross is awarded posthumously, that's one we like to avoid. But, like I said, we got the job done."

With the timing of a television commercial, the waitress returned with their food. Dee wasn't ready to let the conversation end. So she settled her napkin across her lap and asked, "Where were you shot?"

The killer grin returned as Matt picked up his fork. "Why? You want to see my scar?" Before she could answer or remind him that he was again answering a question with a question, he added, "Be careful now, because I'm real particular who I show it to."

He'd skillfully changed the subject from his heroism to his love life, and Dee gave up trying to pry anything else out of him. She laughed in defeat. "I bet."

Matt decided then and there that he liked the sound of her laughter. He also liked the way she'd looked at him while he'd told her about that night. Not like a reporter, but more like a...woman. A woman interested in what he had to say. She was different today, more relaxed than she'd been the night before. Maybe it had something to do with the way she was dressed. Gone was the business suit and, sadly, the skirt that showed off her incredible legs.

But the pair of pressed khaki-colored slacks that hugged her hips made walking behind her a definite privilege. She had a great backside.

"How personal do I have to get in order to view the evidence?" she asked.

Matt took a forkful of rice and red beans, chewed and swallowed before he answered. He wanted to watch her squirm. "How personal do you want to get?"

Dee nearly choked on her salad. She put a hand up as she drew in a breath, obviously unable to speak.

"Don't expire on me. Want me to pound you on the back?"

She shook her head as she regained her composure. "You," she breathed, "are incorrigible."

"Yep, that's what my friends say. Although they might use a slightly different word. Now, about that personal part—"

"Hold it. I've changed my mind. I don't want to get *that* personal."

"Now, there you go again. I told you I'm as harmless as an old dog. I was just gonna say that if you're going to pretend to be my Mz. Right for a day or two, you'll be required to know where my scar is."

She leveled a skeptical gaze at him. "Really? And exactly who is going to quiz me about it? Your mother?"

"Whoa, now there's a low blow. Let's not bring

my mama into this. Trust me, she has absolutely no sense of humor when it comes to my scar and who sees it."

"Good for her. I don't think I would either if I were her."

Matt decided it would be safer to change the subject. "Anyway," he said with exaggerated patience. "Speaking of family, a deal is a deal. I started looking into the old county records this morning concerning your father."

She went all serious on him, and he regretted having to ruin the playful mood. "I've got calls in to several officers who were working that year," he continued. "Two of them are retired and a third is off on leave. It'll probably take a few days of phone tag to catch up with them."

Dee blotted her lips with her napkin. "I scanned the microfiche for old newspapers at the library. I only found one small story about a missing man. It asked anyone who might have seen him to contact the sheriff. That's it. Since we didn't live here, I guess no one was concerned."

"Now, I'm sure that's not true. People disappear all the time for one reason or another. Hell, some folks even think aliens are picking 'em up. Back in those days the sheriff didn't have a computer or any sort of network to track missing persons. They had to rely on witnesses or evidence of foul play. I didn't find a record of either in the files."

"So where do we go from here?"

"I think, Mz. Cates, after we finish lunch, we need to go for a ride."

6

"WHERE DID YOU SAY we're going?"

They'd left the paved road twenty minutes before and had moved steadily into the empty, brush-covered hills surrounding Canyon Lake.

"If we were on horseback, I suppose you could say we're checking the fence line. Sometimes the only way to come up with old information is to look around and ask people. I figure we'll start in the south, travel these roads around the lake and see who we find."

Dee was infinitely grateful that they weren't on horseback. It suited her fine to ride through the empty countryside in the passenger seat with the windows down. A pleasant change from the city streets and traffic of Austin. Besides, it gave her the opportunity to observe Matt in the daylight, without facing his unnerving gaze or his pulse-racing grin.

Wearing a tailored white shirt and tan Western-style slacks, he looked even better than he had the night before. He sat straight behind the wheel with just enough slouch to stay comfortable. He drove with absolute confidence, as if the car were an extension of his body. Under control.

She wondered what it would take to cause him

to lose that control. What kind of woman it would take...

"Last night you said you'd never married because you hadn't found the right woman."

His gaze met hers briefly before returning to the road. "Yeah...?"

"There had to be some runners-up. Hasn't there been someone you *almost* married?"

Matt slowed the car and made a right turn onto a dirt track that looked as if it hadn't been used in at least a year. The first few bumps made Dee brace herself against the door.

"There have been two. I had a serious girlfriend when I was in college. We planned to be married after graduation."

"What happened?"

He leaned back in the seat and propped his elbow against the door. "Spring break during our senior year, she wanted to go to the coast with some friends. I had to work so I stayed home. Nobody's exactly sure what happened. She either got caught in an undertow or had a leg cramp. Anyway, she drowned."

"I'm sorry. That's awful."

Matt pushed his hat back a little. "Yeah, it was pretty bad. I always thought that if I'd been there maybe I could have saved her."

And now he worked at a job trying to save everyone else. "You said two. What happened to the other one."

He smiled, shaking off the past. "That would

be Kristen. She thought I was the one who needed saving."

"From what?"

"From myself I suppose...and my job. Kristen was a career woman whose own career wasn't enough for her. She had some big plans for me, wanted me to quit the Rangers and either go to law school or run for office. I think she had her sights set on the governor's mansion."

"And you didn't want to do that."

"Hell—I mean, heck no. I wanted to be a Ranger since I was twelve years old. Either that or a bank robber. You'd have to know my family to understand, but my dad pretty much quelled that reckless streak when I got old enough to get into trouble. So I ended up becoming a Ranger. I like my job and I'm good at it. I can make a difference, case by case." He paused and looked at Dee. "She was right about me needing to be saved though."

"Really?"

"Yeah. I figured out I needed to be saved from her."

Dee laughed. She couldn't imagine any woman being silly enough to think she could mold this man. He seemed as straight and direct as the long Texas highways he spent so much time traveling.

"Well, here's our first dead end," Matt said and slowed the car.

Up ahead, Dee could see that the track they were following ended at a fence. Instead of turning around, Matt stopped the car. As the dust settled around them, he got out, came around and opened her door.

They were facing west, and the brilliant afternoon sun was partially blocked by huge banks of fluffy white clouds on the horizon. The luminous blue of the sky was breathtaking. Dee squinted and spied three black specks high above the hills dotted with evergreens.

Matt shaded his eyes and looked in the same direction. "Buzzards," he said. He pointed to a tree in the distance. "Look, there's about twenty of them roosting out there."

Dee looked and almost made a wisecrack about the buzzards picking their bones if they got lost. But the old joke failed when the image of her father being watched by buzzards filled her thoughts.

Matt seemed to sense her mood and changed the subject. He faced her with his back to the sun and his arms crossed. "So what about you? Who were your runners-up?"

Although turnabout was fair play, Dee wasn't comfortable talking about her own love life, or lack of one. She'd been badgered enough by her boss and her sister about settling down and getting married. Besides, she needed to keep the time she spent with Matt on a purely professional basis. If she didn't, she had a feeling things could get out of hand.

Way out of hand.

She had no intention of complicating her life with a man—especially a man whose picture had appeared in *Texas Men Magazine*, willingly or not. "I've been a little too busy to do any running," she said, dodging the bullet.

"Too busy? Are the men in Austin that slow?"

Dee crossed her arms and leaned back against the fender of Matt's car. She mentally drew her defenses around her and resettled into her familiar, safe, control mode. Might as well tell him the truth and get it over with. No use getting emotional about it.

"I learned a long time ago not to base my life on a man." He started to speak, and she put a hand up to stop him. "I've dated...still date now and then, for that matter. But I devote most of my time to my career."

"Did you learn that from your father?"

"What?"

"That you couldn't depend on a man."

Again Matt went straight to the heart of the matter. *No digging allowed.* She had to protect her heart at all cost. She'd taught herself to keep her distance. It was the only legacy her father had left her. "Didn't anyone ever tell you that some things are none of your business?"

"All the time," he answered. "Doesn't keep me from asking though. Rangers get paid to be nosy. I'm probably the nosiest one you're likely to meet. So? Is this about your father?"

With a sigh Dee gave up. She hadn't talked openly to anyone about her father in years, yet it seemed appropriate to discuss him with Matt.

She didn't want to examine the implications of that fact.

"I suppose so," she said carefully. "I learned that whatever a man can give, he can also take away. Whether it's financial support, emotional support, or love. If you depend on another person, you'll be disappointed." Inwardly, Dee winced at the cold sound of her own words.

"Whew!" Matt uncrossed his arms and balanced them on his hips. "So you don't depend on anyone for anything?"

"It's not a good idea."

"How can you be so sure?"

"I've watched my mother shut down her life after my father disappeared. I don't intend to let that happen to me."

Dee felt the heat rise in her neck, and it had nothing to do with the bright sunshine. She'd never uttered those words to anyone but her sister. Suddenly, she felt too naked, too vulnerable, facing the frowning man in front of her.

"What do you tell the men who are interested in you for more than just a date or two?"

Pent-up emotion bubbled through Dee. She had to clear her throat to answer. "I tell them I'm too busy, because I am." She raised her chin and dared him to argue with her. She had to get back on solid footing, and the only way she knew to do that was to take control. "Right now we're supposed to be looking for clues about my father. I don't think we're going to find them here." She turned before he could answer and got into the car.

Matt blew out a breath to release the tightness in his chest as he watched her take her seat. He'd wanted to disagree with her, to make her see that she had to depend on someone, sometime. But it hadn't worked. He rubbed a hand down his face and moved toward the driver's side of the car. He was losing his cool. Arguing wasn't his style. How did she manage to rile him up by simply making a statement she believed in?

Because he didn't want her to believe it. He wanted her to know she could depend on him. But the only way to prove it seemed to be tracking her father. If he could dig up some clues, maybe he could change her mind. Put the past to rest. Mend a part of her heart that had been broken by the most important man in her life.

He got in, started the car and turned it around. Dee stayed silent, looking out the window, shutting him out for now. That was okay. They had work to do.

THREE HOURS and about a hundred and fifty miles later, they called it a day. They'd stopped at several isolated ranches and every gas station or store on the southern side of the lake. Asking questions. Looking for any establishment or old-timer that might have been in the area eighteen years ago.

He'd kept the afternoon strictly business and after a while Dee had loosened up. Now that she'd relaxed, he didn't want to let her go quite so soon.

As they pulled up to a stoplight headed back toward the main highway, Matt had another idea. And it suited him in more ways than one.

"How about I show you one of our local traditions. There's a little town south of here on the way back to San Antone that you might like to see. Ever been to Gruene?"

When Dee said she hadn't, Matt made a right at the light instead of getting on the highway. The road wound through flat farmland with an occasional house here and there. Dee seemed to perk up when they cruised onto the main street of Gruene.

The setting sun gave the rustic buildings of the town a picturesque look. Antique shabbiness transformed by warm light into an impressionist's dream.

"What a pretty place," Dee said. "A friend of mine came through here and told me about this town. I just never made it down this way."

Matt stepped into the opening she'd just given him. "Don't tell me, let me guess. You were too busy."

Dee looked at him frowning, but when he jokingly ducked in case she tried to hit him, she smiled.

Then she hit him...flat-handed, on the shoulder.

"Yes, exactly," she agreed, settling back in her seat and crossing her arms.

Matt had to laugh. He also had to look away or he would have pulled her toward him, playfully of course, and paid her back by kissing her. *Pay attention here, sport*, he warned himself. *Don't put the cart before the horse.* He knew she wasn't ready to be kissed. But that didn't stop him from wishing she was.

There were only two paved roads in the little town. Matt paused at the crossroads for a little longer than necessary to give Dee a chance to look around. Then he turned into a parking spot in front of a big wooden building that looked like an old, weathered barn. The carved sign on the front said Gruene Dance Hall.

"Here we are," he announced as he shut off the engine. Dee was already unbuckling her seat belt.

"I thought we'd take a break. Maybe have a beer," Matt said as he met Dee in front of the car. "But, if you want, we could walk around a little before it gets dark."

Dee wanted to walk. It had been a long time since she'd played tourist, and this quaint little town intrigued her. In some ways it felt as if they'd stepped back in time. "Thanks," she said. "I'd like that."

They walked down one side of the street and up the other. There were souvenir shops, artists displaying pottery and jewelry, and of course, antique shops.

"This doesn't seem like a place you'd spend a lot of time in," she said as they peered in the window of a closed outdoor-outfitting store. She met his gaze in the reflection of the window, waiting for his answer.

"Can't truthfully say that it is," he answered. "I stop over at the dance hall once in a while, just to keep in touch. It has a long history in this county and most of the people around here come by for sentimental reasons." He touched her back lightly to turn her toward the hall. "Besides, it's as good a place as any to ask questions."

Still being the Ranger, Dee thought in disappointment as his hand fell away from her back. She had to figure out a way to keep him from touching her. She was beginning to like it too much and that realization was a dangerous surprise. Why did Matt's touch override her usual defenses? She'd recently watched a documentary on genetic messengers and pheromones. Maybe it all came down to hormones after all, she thought wryly, like fish and frogs. Well, she could even resist chemistry as long as she kept her wits about her. And as long as Matt kept his hands to himself.

They crossed the road and Matt opened the door for her to enter the dance hall. "Are Rangers *always* on duty?" Dee asked.

"Officially? No," he answered. "Unofficially, yes. It's that kind of job. I do have one rule I always follow though," he said as the rickety wooden screen door closed behind them. "I never drink beer when I'm wearin' my gun."

Matt nodded to the balding, thirty-something man behind the bar as they approached the line of stools. "Barry," he acknowledged as he took Dee's arm to settle her on a seat.

"Hey, Matt. How are you doin'?"

"Better than I oughta be," Matt replied. He remained standing next to her. "This is Mz. Dee Cates from the television station in Austin—KAUS."

"Nice to meet you," Barry replied.

"Same here," Dee said and extended her hand. Barry wiped his on his apron before taking hers. Then, after a brief shake, he got back to business. "What can I get for you?"

"I'll have a bourbon and water, without the bourbon," Matt said. "And the lady will have…?"

"Beer," Dee said. "Whatever you have on draft."

"Comin' up."

As they waited for their drinks, Dee glanced around the room. There weren't many people inside and the place seemed a little forlorn. The walls at the front of the hall were covered with photographs of all the music acts and comedians who had entertained over the years. There were familiar faces like Willie Nelson, and less familiar ones like the Amarillo Hot Peppers.

"It's a tradition for Texas musicians to play Gruene Hall," Matt told her. "Most of them have been here at one time or another."

Dee sipped her beer and read one name after another. When she spied a picture of John Travolta, she had to get off her stool and go investigate. Matt followed her.

"John Travolta was here?" she asked. "Why?"

"Remember the movie *Michael?*"

"Of course," she answered.

"Remember the part in the dance hall?"

"Sure, it was my favorite part of the movie," Dee said.

"Well, they filmed that here." He turned to indicate the big empty, wood-plank dance floor behind the bar.

"That must have been interesting," she said, walking closer to the entrance.

"The people around here enjoyed it."

"I would have enjoyed it." Dee sighed, pressing a hand to her heart like a lovesick teenager. "John Travolta in the flesh."

Matt did the guy thing and simply rolled his eyes. "You're too busy, remember?"

The outer door opened at that moment and several couples entered the bar. Matt again touched Dee to guide her back to the bar. *Careful...* She should tell him to stop it before she got used to his touch, she decided, but then his hand slid away when she reached her seat. She'd tell him in no uncertain terms next time, though.

After the bartender had taken care of the newcomers, Matt called him over again.

"I'm lookin' for an old-timer who knows this county. Anybody come to mind?"

Barry leaned against the bar and frowned. "Let

me think... What kind of information you lookin' for?"

"It's a missing-person's case, so I need somebody who used to travel the backcountry around the lake. You know, hunters, fishermen. The case is around twenty years old."

"Hey, Barry!" someone called from down the bar. "Let me have some change for the juke."

Barry raised a hand in acknowledgment but remained where he was. "My dad might know somebody." He tapped the bar as he turned to deliver the change. "I'll give him a call and ask."

"Thanks," Matt said.

Soon the jukebox was belting out one of Garth Brooks's honky-tonk songs and two of the couples were dancing. Dee couldn't help tapping her feet in time to the music.

"They have live bands on the weekends. You should see this place on a Friday night," Matt said. "You can hardly get on the dance floor."

"I bet," Dee said as she watched the dancers two-step the long length of the wood-plank floor.

"Do people dance much up in Austin or are they all too busy, like you?"

Dee narrowed her eyes. "Do Texas Rangers dance? Or are they too busy being smart as—"

"Whoa!" He put up a hand to stop her. "I thought you'd never ask." He grinned. Then he took her hand.

Before Dee could figure out how he'd maneuvered her into this, she was dancing...in the arms of Matt Travis, the Lone Star Lover.

And it felt good. That was the scary thing. When they reached the floor, they easily glided into a two-step as if they'd been dancing together for years.

"I guess somewhere along the way, you had time to learn to dance," Matt said, still teasing her.

"I'm a transplanted Texan, after all," she replied in the haughtiest voice she could muster while smiling.

"I thought you might be one of those 'progressive'-music types."

"I like some of that too," she answered. "And rock." Dee knew she was babbling but being in Matt's arms, feeling their bodies moving in rhythm, his warm hand clasping hers made her more than nervous. Their proximity was close to driving her crazy. "You make 'progressive' sound like a dirty word," she managed to say, trying to keep her mind on the subject—music.

"We've already ascertained the fact that I'm a fairly traditional kind of guy," he answered.

The song was ending. Dee decided it was a good thing, too. But as the last notes died, they ended up at the far end of the floor. Instead of crossing the distance, they stopped, waiting for the next song.

It was a slow dance.

Matt didn't grin. However, he *did* watch her face as he pulled her close. What she saw in his eyes made her heart take several hard, panicked beats. As he guided her head to his shoulder so his hat wouldn't bump her, she felt more than heard him draw in a breath.

Suddenly, Dee knew they were in big trouble.

They seemed to be touching everywhere, although that wasn't possible. The warmth of his arms and chest seeped into her and made her exquisitely aware of how well they fit together. The slow, sure movements of his body guiding hers made Dee want to close her eyes and float in any direction he led her.

And she could smell him. His shirt, his skin smelled faintly of soap, of aftershave and of male. When her forehead bumped his chin, she felt the slight rasp of day-old whiskers. The friction sent a shiver of sensation down her spine. She would stop this soon, she decided dreamily. She would get everything back under control in a few moments. But until then she moved closer, wanting to feel more of him, more of the craziness running through her.

"I could get used to this," Matt murmured close to her ear.

"Me too," Dee said, and sighed.

7

MATT COULDN'T BELIEVE his ears. He tugged Dee a little closer. "What was that?"

Dee's body tightened slightly as if he'd surprised her. "Hmm? What?"

"Did you say something?"

Instead of answering, she shook her head without looking at him.

Matt decided he must be coming down with a bad case of wishful thinking. He thought she'd said… Well, no matter, he could still enjoy holding her, even if she didn't feel the same way.

He wanted her to relax again. He loosened his arms slightly, expecting her to move away, but she didn't. So he took the opportunity to breathe in the scent of her. Her hair smelled like strawberries or raspberries, something sweet. Under that was the pure essence of woman. The thought of pushing his face into her hair and nuzzling her ear caused him to miss a step.

Dee lost the rhythm of the dance and glanced up at him questioningly.

Damn.

"Sorry about that," he said, feeling more uncoordinated than a fifteen-year-old at his first dance lesson. The song played out the last notes as he gazed down at her. He'd run out of time. His feet stopped dancing, but his arms didn't let her go.

She smiled a sweet, almost shy smile and said, "Thank you."

Now he wouldn't have pegged Mz. Dee Cates, the TV lady, as being shy. Not once. But looking down into her smoky blue eyes and seeing part of the woman underneath the shield she kept between her and other people made his chest tighten. He wanted to tell her she didn't need to hide with him, but he couldn't. He didn't have the right unless she gave it to him. "You're welcome," he said, unable to think of anything else.

When a few people at the bar started to applaud, he had to let her go. He kept his hand on her back though, to cross the dance floor to the bar. The jukebox kicked into another two-step as Dee took her seat.

Matt needed all his willpower to train his gaze on Barry leaning against his side of the bar. If Matt looked at Dee, he might do or say something he'd regret.

"I called my dad and asked him about what he remembered," Barry said. "He mentioned a guy who used to roam around this part of the county, an old-timer they used to see most often when they went hunting on the eastern side of the lake toward the river. Dad said the guy lived out there somewhere. He'd scavenge around looking for arrowheads or whatever he could find. Huntin' for a little piece of history to sell." Barry shrugged. "There was a story going around about an old bandit treasure supposedly buried near the river. Maybe that's what he wanted. Anyway, Dad hasn't seen him in years. The old guy might even be dead by now. Anyway, if you need to call my dad, here's his number."

"Thanks, Barry," Matt said as he took the card. "I'll check it out." Finally, he felt calm enough to face Dee. "Are you ready to go?"

She'd changed back into the career woman—all business. The person he'd glimpsed on the dance floor was well hidden. He didn't like the change worth a damn, but for now it was probably safer for them both.

"Sure. Are we going to look for him tonight?" she asked as she slid off the stool.

The idea of walking around with Dee in the dark brought back the sensation of having her in his arms again on the dance floor.

"No, not tonight," he managed to say.

That was about the last coherent thought Matt had, because by the time they reached the car, he went completely brain dead. He figured his granny would have been highly disappointed in him, even though Dee hadn't seemed to mind.

It was an accident. He'd walked her to the passenger side of the car, opened the door and waited for her to get in. But the breeze blew the door just enough to nudge him into her. Then nature took its course.

Before he could say "Excuse me," they were

bumping noses. She didn't slap him, and he couldn't walk away without tasting her.

BUMPING NOSES with Matt would have been funny, Dee thought dreamily, if kissing him hadn't felt so good. When his mouth had descended to meet hers she only had one thought— she wanted to be kissed. No laughing matter.

And he kissed her. His warm breath fanned across her cheek then his lips teased hers, taking a tantalizing taste of her mouth before moving away. Asking a question that, as she gazed up into his eyes, she realized she couldn't afford to answer. Not then, not now. His hand slid in a leisurely caress along her spine and the nervousness she'd first felt around him returned with a vengeance, mixed with heat. Controlling the situation seemed impossible.

Then Matt backed off before she could surrender.

"I'm sorry," he said. "I didn't mean—"

Dee shook her head to stop the apology. She was still struggling with her body's hot, hedonistic response to his inquiring mouth. She wanted to kiss him again, to melt into his arms without thinking, letting him take them where they both wanted to go.

His apology brought her back to her senses. She knew he hadn't intended to corner her. But she wasn't about to let him see how deeply a single kiss had affected her. She needed Matt to help her find out about the past. She couldn't allow him into her future, no matter how much she wanted him in the present. She groped for her sense of humor, for a way to diffuse the situation.

"That's okay, cowboy. Just don't let it happen again." She watched as Matt drew in a slow breath before narrowing his eyes.

"Did you just call me a cowboy?" he asked, as if he'd been highly insulted.

As much as a part of Dee regretted it, they were back on common...safer ground. "Must be the hat," she added. Her voice still sounded a little shaky so she slid into the car. She had to get out of range of his gaze and his dangerous mouth before he caught the scent of her struggle, and called her on it.

They didn't say much on the way back to San Antonio. Dee decided it was better that way. Not as enjoyable, but better. She needed some time out. Being with Matt had somehow gotten her off course. She didn't have time to dance with or be kissed by a man she'd set up for an interview. No matter how strongly she might be attracted to him. She had to remind herself that Matt was the Lone Star Lover, and that mixing business with pleasure wasn't her style.

"You want to stop for some dinner before I take you back?" he asked.

The sun had gone down while they were in the dance hall, and Dee realized she had no idea what time it was. Hunger, however, wasn't her first concern.

"No. It's been a long day. I think I'll go to the

hotel, order room service and take a long, hot bath."

It was several moments before Matt spoke again. "About tomorrow, then. I have to stop by my office for an hour or so, make some calls and check on a few things. Do you want to meet for lunch again, then ride out and look for Barry's old-timer?"

Dee thought it best to keep the time they socialized to a minimum, at least for her own peace of mind. She was already breaking her golden rule by depending on him to investigate her father's disappearance. She didn't want to make a habit of depending on him for entertainment, too. "Let's make it after lunch. I need to do some shopping. I didn't bring enough clothes for a week and I can't wear my business suit to go hiking through the brush." *When in doubt, go shopping.*

He nodded once without taking his gaze from the road. Things didn't get awkward until they reached the restaurant where she'd left her car. This wasn't a date, she reminded herself. They were both professionals. If he hadn't kissed her, they'd be able to shake hands and say good-night. Now she didn't know what to do. So instead of waiting for him to open her door when they arrived, Dee opened it herself and got out, effectively putting the door between them. The slight frown on his face broadcast his disapproval and Dee winced. It wasn't that she didn't trust him...it was her own self-control that was in doubt.

"Well, thanks for an interesting afternoon," she said, aiming for a brisk businesslike tone.

"You're welcome," he said slowly. "Maybe next time we'll do better toward finding something out."

"Maybe," she said in agreement, then immediately felt like an ungrateful witch. "Listen, Ranger—I mean, Matt. I really appreciate your help..." He didn't speak so she stumbled on. "You've spent so much time already..."

Matt crossed his arms. "I told you, it's my job." He held her immobilized with his gaze. "Now, the kissing part, that was something else all together. I'll apologize again if you want me to. And if you're worried about being alone with me—"

"I'm not worried." She couldn't stand the thought of him taking the blame for something neither of them had planned. And for something she'd enjoyed. She closed the car door behind her, removing the barrier between them. "What time tomorrow?"

"How does one o'clock sound, right here?" he asked as he walked with her to her car.

"That's fine," she answered.

He didn't try to open her door this time, but he did close it after she got in, and waited for her to start the engine. As she pulled out of the lot, she looked in the rearview mirror and saw him watching her as he walked back to his car.

Later that evening, as she relaxed in a hot bath after picking up her messages and eating her dinner, Dee's mind went over the events of the day and the way it had ended. She was glad he hadn't tried to kiss her again, wasn't she?

Well, not exactly. But things were better this way. Matt seemed willing enough to help her find out about her father. But anything beyond that would only complicate matters. And her life was complicated enough. Just the messages she had after one day proved that. She'd had one from her boss, two from her assistant and another from the manager of the Dating Corral.

Would the guy *ever* give up?

Suddenly, she remembered the dance she and Matt had shared, the brief taste of him when he'd brushed her lips with his and she felt hot all over again. And it had nothing to do with the temperature of the bathwater.

MATT LISTENED to the phone ring and debated whether to answer it or not. The last two times he'd given in, he'd had to explain to two complete strangers why he wasn't on the marriage market anymore, when he hadn't ever really been on the market in the first place.

On top of that, he'd just walked in the door after leaving Dee and wasn't in the mood for conversation with anyone right then. He'd thought of all the things he could have said on the drive home. Things like how much he'd enjoyed dancing with her, how well they'd fit together. How the taste of her mouth had set his body off—

What if it was Dee trying to get him? On the

sixth ring, he picked up the receiver. "Hello?" He knew his voice sounded gruff but he didn't care much at the moment. He could think of several ways to apologize to Dee later if it happened to be her.

"Hello, Matthew?"

Matt pushed away his lascivious thoughts. "Hi, Mom."

"Don't 'hi' me. I've been calling you all afternoon. Is your answering machine broken?"

Matt glanced at the machine he'd gutted the night before. "Yes, it is. You should have tried my pager. Is something wrong?"

"I didn't want to bother you at work. It wasn't an emergency. Nothing is wrong…yet."

Yet. He could tell by his mother's tone of voice she was het up about something. He also had no doubt she'd tell him in her own good time.

"I got a call from your brother Nathan this afternoon. He said that Bill Hazard told him you were serious about a woman from a television station."

Matt closed his eyes and imagined about three different ways he could dismember Bill Hazard. Leave it to him to go for the jugular by getting Matt's family involved. His mother had been after him for years to settle down and have a family like his two brothers. And she wasn't a woman to cross.

"Well," he began to explain, then stopped. He couldn't say it was all a big joke. And he'd never been good at lying, especially to his mother. He'd learned early on it was better to be whipped for the truth than to be caught in a lie. "Not exactly," he hedged. Even as he said it, he realized the sad part was, he could get serious about Dee Cates real easy. That idea set him back. He didn't need to get involved with a "too busy" career woman who'd be out of his life in three or four days.

"What does 'not exactly' mean? Bill told Nathan that you said she was Miss Right."

"Well, I did sort of say that, but—"

"When were you going to get around to introducing her to your family? After the wedding?"

"Now, Mom, you know better than that. I've only known her for—"

"Sunday."

"What?"

"Bring her out here on Sunday. Your dad will cook up some steaks and ribs. She can meet the whole family."

Matt rubbed the bridge of his nose with his free hand. This joke thing was about to give him a headache. The idea of Dee meeting his family wasn't so outlandish. Actually, it might just serve her right. He'd be the butt of every joke in town once her story about dating was broadcast. He figured if she could interview a barful of women who were after his hide, then meeting his family shouldn't slow her down. Posing as his future bride might be a stretch, but Dee ought to be able to handle it.

"I don't know, Mom, I'll have to ask her about it."

"I understand. But tell her we're counting on her."

"Sure. I'll tell her."

"See you Sunday," she said and hung up.

Matt broke the connection and immediately dialed Bill Hazard's pager number. It was about time he put a stop to this nonsense. By the time Matt reached the point in the message where he had to punch in his number so Bill could call him back, he realized he was making a mistake. He hung up the phone. Confronting Bill would only make things worse. Bill would know he was winning. Better to let him wonder about the truth.

As had been regularly the case for the last day and a half, Dee Cates hijacked his thoughts. Matt forgot about what he should or shouldn't tell Bill Hazard. He had a bigger problem. What was he going to tell Dee?

8

"YOU'RE QUIETER than usual," Dee remarked.

They'd been driving for thirty minutes and the silence between her and Matt was beginning to get on her nerves. He'd proven to be the strong, but not particularly silent type, and she missed his teasing.

"I have some things on my mind, that's all." He angled a smile in her direction. "Did you find everything you needed on your shopping trip?"

"Of course." She returned his smile. "I found a mall. I bought two outfits and a pair of boots. That should last me until I leave." Dee pulled up a few inches of the hem of the long skirt she wore and angled her foot to the middle of the floorboard to show off her new low-heeled Justins. "See? These should be a little better for walking on rocks."

"I expect so," Matt said. "Although helping you over the rocks the other night didn't bother me a bit."

Well, it bothered me, Dee added silently as she dropped her hem back into place. *Keep it professional*, she reminded herself. *Don't let him know that he's affecting you, that his kiss was the last thing you thought about as you drifted off to sleep.* She didn't want Matt asking for more than she could give, did she?

"I would've thought you'd buy a pair of jeans," he said, looking disappointed.

"I'm more comfortable in a skirt for walking, or shorts. Jeans are for riding horses," she informed him.

"So, where are we headed today?" she asked, sticking to a safe subject. She'd assumed they would cover more of the territory they'd been in the day before. But even a tourist would know they were driving south toward Corpus Christi, the opposite direction of Canyon Lake.

Matt leaned back slightly and rested his left arm on the edge of the window before answering. "What's the matter, don't you trust me?"

Dee was more worried about trusting herself. She managed to raise an eyebrow and give him her best sardonic look. "Why, Mr. Lone Star, why ever would you think that?"

Instead of being cowed, he chuckled before filling her in. "Well, I got a hold of one of the Rangers in the area, James Dillworth. Thought we'd stop by and talk to him, maybe see what he remembers about that time. Then we'll go from there to the lake and start on the eastern side, where that old-timer used to roam around. It's a slim chance, but he might still be living out there."

Dee suddenly realized she was feeling way too complacent about the investigation. She'd never let anyone plan out her days before. Even her program director stopped short of going further than scheduling her on-air time and deadlines. Why was she allowing Matt Travis to take over?

"You know?" she said. "It might be better if we split up. We could cover more ground that way."

Matt looked at her for a long moment, then shifted his gaze back to the road. "You may not know it, but I think you've got more answers in you than questions. I'm hoping to stumble onto the right question, and I'm counting on you to recognize the right answer."

Dee couldn't argue with that. In the past she'd spent time asking questions and had come up with nothing. She'd started this investigation by asking for his help. She'd be a fool not to follow it through simply out of pride...or nerve.

"Okay, Kemo Sabe. You lead, I follow." *For now.*

ABOUT FORTY MINUTES LATER, Matt slowed the car and turned into the arched gateway framed by two gnarled evergreens that said A&J Ranch. Several barking dogs raced up the long dirt driveway to meet them. As he brought the car to a stop, a tall man wearing a Stetson stepped out onto the porch of a modest, but neatly kept Spanish-style ranch house.

"Afternoon, James," Matt said as stepped out of the car.

"Donner! Meg! Quiet down," the man admonished the dogs as he came down the stairs to greet them. Matt opened the door for Dee and touched her back as he guided her forward. His touch had her thinking of being in his arms again as she had been last night when they'd danced. She hesitated slightly, confused by the strength of the memory and the wanting... Then Matt's hand fell away, taking the warmth out of her fantasy. James nodded in his direction before he settled his gaze on Dee.

Looking into his weathered face, Dee initially thought he must be at least eighty years old, but then she got close enough to see his eyes. They were clear and blue like her own, and sparkling with a sharp, observant intelligence.

"Dee Cates, this is Ranger Jim Dillworth," Matt said.

Ranger Dillworth tipped his hat to her and smiled. "He left the retired part off that introduction," he said, although he seemed pleased by the omission. "Nice to meet you, Miss Cates. Come on in. My Ann is fixing us some lemonade."

In very short order they were introduced to Ann Dillworth and settled at the kitchen table sipping homemade lemonade.

"Yep, there aren't many retired Rangers around," Jim said, continuing the conversation they'd begun outside. "Most of them die with their badge on." He glanced toward his wife. "But me, I came up with a bum ticker. I decided to let the young bucks take over so I could do a little more fishin' before I die." He paused briefly, settled back into his chair and asked, "Now, what can I do for you folks?"

Dee allowed Matt to fill Ranger Dillworth in on the few details they had about her father. He asked several questions about the officer of record, and the actual location the car had been found, then he turned to Dee.

"I know you had to be a child at the time, but how much do you know about your father?"

"Well, I remember him as being happy. He loved to take us on family trips." She remembered how many times she and her sister, Jeanie, had posed by a "Welcome to—" sign so her father could take their picture.

"Have you found out anything else about him since? Has your mother ever mentioned any problems?" James asked.

The image of her father holding a camera and smiling disappeared. Dee could only stare at Ranger Dillworth. "What do you mean?"

He raised a hand in a placating gesture. "Now don't get insulted. I'm just asking you to think about your father from an adult's perspective instead of a child's. Parents don't always tell their kids about problems in a marriage."

"You're saying he might have disappeared because he wanted to?"

Ranger Dillworth sighed but held her gaze. "Unfortunately, that's a common occurrence."

Dee couldn't deny that the idea of desertion had crossed her mind. "I did ask my mother whether he was happy with us. Of course she said yes. But then, ever since he disappeared, she's acted as though he might come back any day."

"Did she ever say where she thought he was headed that morning?"

"No, she doesn't like to talk about it. I remember him leaving, though. He was going out to hunt for Indian relics. Arrowheads and pieces of pottery. He had a whole collection of things he'd found on our other trips. He especially loved the pieces of pottery with blue in the design. He said they were the rarest. He used to let me help him catalog them." Her father's collection was still neatly boxed and shelved in her mother's basement. Dee felt a sudden rush of sadness for all they'd missed doing together over the years. "He said he'd be back for supper."

"Well…" Ranger Dillworth looked from Dee to Matt. "I don't remember the actual case. I would imagine at the time they did at least a cursory search of the area. Especially since his wallet was found in the glove compartment of the car. But there are plenty of places to get lost, or to come to a bad end in that rocky terrain. A hard area to search, perfect for rattlesnakes." He shook his head in resignation. "I wish I could be of more help to you."

Matt spoke up. "I heard there used to be an old-timer who scavenged in those hills. Did you ever run across anybody like that?"

"Let me think." He scratched his chin. "Yep, you're right. There was an old, raggedy guy everybody called Tinker. Tinker Evans. He used to collect junk, empty bullet cartridges and such.

Sold them to the old Alligator Creek trading post for food. Was he listed as a witness?"

"No, not officially. I've been askin' around, trying to dig up the name of someone who might have been in that area at the time. The trading post burned to the ground over ten years ago."

"Well, I doubt if old Tinker is still around," James said. "Seems like he was pushin' a hundred back then. 'Course, it could have been hard livin' that made him look older. If I remember correctly, he stayed on the Hayes County side of the lake in one of the deeper canyons. More desolate over there, even now."

Matt stood and picked up his hat from the table. "I really appreciate your help," he said.

Dee felt his calming touch again as he indicated for her to stand. "Yes, thank you for your time," she said, and extended her hand.

Ranger Dillworth smiled as his large, work-roughened hand engulfed hers. "Well, I didn't help much, but the pleasure was all mine. Helping a lady in distress is the best kind of assignment. Right, Matt?"

"Yes, sir," Matt answered. "No doubt about that."

On the way out, they thanked Ann Dillworth for the refreshments. Ann and James stood arm in arm on the porch as they drove away.

"How long do you suppose they've been together?" Dee asked.

"Oh, probably about fifty years," Matt answered. "People in these parts tend to marry young and stay together, as a rule."

Dee glanced back at the couple who had been united through fifty years of everything the world could throw at them. A fresh streak of sadness opened inside her and just for a moment she envied them. How did one go about finding the right someone to love and be loved by for fifty years? Dee had no idea. She hoped her sister had found that kind of love. Jeanie had married her college sweetheart and now had three kids. She'd been after Dee for years to slow down with her career and find the right man.

Then Dee thought of her mother and how long she'd been alone. And how long she'd lived with the silent judgment by others that she was an abandoned wife. She'd thought she'd found the right man—Dee's father. Then he'd simply disappeared one day. No wonder her mother had stopped discussing it years ago.

"Do you think my father just walked away and left us?"

Matt took several seconds to formulate his answer. "I'm inclined to believe your memory of the situation. If there had been problems in the marriage, you would have heard hard words or seen your mother crying. Twelve is old enough to recognize trouble."

For some reason, Dee felt relieved by his statement. She understood that outsiders would automatically assume the worst about people, because so many people lived up to that expectation. But she'd wanted Matt to believe otherwise, to give her father the benefit of the doubt, as she'd always tried to do.

She looked over at him. "Thank you."

He glanced in her direction and awarded her his killer grin. Dee's heart struggled through several pounding beats before he answered.

"You're welcome."

THEY'D BEEN WALKING for at least an hour. Dee was beginning to regret her faith in her new boots. Thank goodness the late-summer air in the foothills remained cool. They'd followed an old wagon road into the hills on the eastern side of Canyon Lake until the road gave out. Then they'd followed a footpath that looked promising. But that had disappeared into the rocky shoulders of the hills. Standing on top of one of the lower ledges, Dee glanced back the way they'd come. She could barely make out the roof of Matt's car in the distance. The hike that seemed to have taken forever hadn't gotten them very far.

Matt checked around a boulder for what he called "critters," then instructed her to sit.

"I'm gonna walk on up to the top and see what's on the other side. Be right back."

Dee didn't argue. After the first thirty minutes of walking, she realized how much of a city girl she'd become. Her television job had kept her mostly indoors and in the dark. But now her feet were broadcasting their own signals. She briefly thought of removing her new boots to wiggle her toes but thought better of it. She might not be able to get them back on.

When Matt's footsteps faded away, Dee was caught by the silence all around her. No cars, no planes, no voices…just the occasional call of a bird and the whispering of the wind.

Drawing in a deep breath of cooler air filled with the scent of ancient evergreen trees stunted by the hardscrabble terrain, she sighed. Then she shaded her eyes and looked toward the lowering sun.

This would be a place to get lost in, a quiet, solitary place to think or escape the harsh realities of living. Had her father walked over these same hills? Had he found whatever he'd been searching for? Looking out over miles of empty countryside, she had to admit that the odds of finding anything related to her father's disappearance were slim to none. It was beginning to look as if she'd never know.

Several minutes later, she heard Matt's footsteps long before she saw him. He squatted next to her, but his gaze traveled to the sun on the horizon. He glanced at his watch.

"We're gonna run out of sun soon," he said as he pushed his hat back to glance at Dee.

Looking directly into his eyes at close range always startled her. The last time she'd done it, she'd just been kissed. She forced her thoughts back to the present dilemma.

"We seem to be coming up dry anyway. This

whole thing is probably a wild-goose chase," she said, willing to let him off the hook.

"I would have said the same thing twenty minutes ago, but not now." He raised a hand and pointed upward. "At the top of this ridge there's a marker, a pile of rocks like the old prospectors used to use to mark their claims."

"What does that mean?"

He shook his head. "It might mean nothin'. There's no way to tell how long it's been there. Could be a year, could be ten years. But it's a sign that someone claimed this land, or marked it to keep people out. Someone who knew the old ways."

Dee pushed to her feet and grimaced. Matt rose also and put out a hand to steady her.

"Let's go check it out then," she said.

He stopped her. "Not today. And not on foot. I'm gonna call a guy I know who does aerial surveys. It's going to take some horse power to search this area right."

"What kind of vehicle can drive through these hills?" Dee asked in disbelief.

Matt's grin widened. "I'm talking about real, old-time horse power—as in horses."

At that moment, with her feet throbbing, the thought of riding a horse seemed like an excellent idea. She didn't even mind that Matt was standing there laughing at her for being such a city slicker.

"Sounds great, where do we get the horses?"

He crossed his arms and narrowed his eyes in

what Dee had decided to call his "just a minute there missy" face. "I'll provide the horses. Do you know how to ride?" he asked.

"I'll have you know I did a story on rodeo barrel riders, and part of it was interviewer participation," she huffed, crossing her own arms. "Yes, cowboy, I was raised in Texas. I know how to ride."

Matt laughed and took her arm. "There you go again, callin' me a cowboy." He guided her toward the trail back to the car then fell in step behind her. "Just remember, there's more to me than my hat."

Matt watched Dee walk in front of him and figured he had to be about the luckiest son of a...gun in the county right then. She was a woman used to taking the lead, and in this instance, he didn't mind one bit. Unlike those too-slow men in Austin, he could keep up with her. And even though she wasn't wearin' those nicely fitted pants she'd had on the day before, or a nice pair of tight jeans, the sway of her hips in the loose-fitting skirt was reward enough for a dusty day in the middle of nowhere.

The farther they went, however, the more gingerly she stepped. Finally, when they were within sight of the car, he stopped her. "Are you okay?"

She pulled a face that would have been cute if it hadn't worried him.

"It's my new boots. Bad idea to go hiking when they weren't broken in."

He looked down at her feet, then toward the car. "Can you make it?"

"What are my choices?" she asked then smiled. "Of course I can make it. I'm just a little slower than when we started."

"I can carry you," he said. Before she could protest, he bent and lifted her off the ground.

"What are you doing?" Dee gasped in surprise. "You'll hurt yourself."

Matt chuckled. "I don't think so. I've hauled things a lot heavier than you." He didn't mind at all. Having her in his arms would be reward enough for the physical effort of helping her up the last hill.

Her face was close enough for him to see the conflicting thoughts running through her mind. He just let her run on. She'd have to squirm out of his arms to get away, 'cause he wasn't gonna put her down and watch her limp. After a few seconds she seemed to settle, but she wouldn't give in yet. She rolled her eyes and sighed. "Oh, please, let's not get out of hand with this damsel-in-distress thing. It's not much farther."

"No, it's not," Matt agreed and started walking again, not taking the time to convince her.

Carrying her turned out to be more torture than he'd expected, but not because she was heavy. He'd forgotten how having Dee in his arms affected him. He could feel the warmth of her skin through her clothes, and for the first time he agreed with her decision to wear a soft skirt instead of jeans. The flutter of her breath on his neck sent shivers of sensation under his skin. She smelled like sunshine, strawberries and dust, and he wanted to dip his head and taste her lips.

He kept his eyes on the trail however, and Dee stayed perfectly still, impersonating a bale of hay, he supposed. Unfortunately, he could feel her heartbeat against his chest and through the palms of his hands. And the fast rhythm of her pulse made his throat go dry. He swallowed and kept walking.

When they reached the car, Matt allowed Dee's feet to slide to the ground, bringing them face-to-face. For a moment he toyed with the idea of kissing her, but he held back when he saw her wince. He reined in his libido and brought his mind back to the problem at hand. He decided to check her feet first.

Matt placed his palm on the hood of the car and found it cool to the touch. The late-afternoon sun lacked the heat of midday. With one smooth motion he put his hands on her hips and boosted her up.

"Let's take a look," he said then lifted her right foot and removed the boot. "Do you have any blisters?"

She pulled her foot away, looking nervous. "I don't think so. Listen, I'm not a horse that's gone lame. I'm simply wearing a new pair of boots and they hurt."

"Well, you're about as skittish as a fractious mare," he accused as he trapped her foot once more. "I'm not going to do anything indecent, just relax a minute. The best thing for sore feet, in people and in horses, is to increase the blood flow." He checked her heel and then her toes before kneading the ball of her foot.

She drew in a sharp breath. "Ow."

"Too hard?" He hesitated.

"No, it—" She leaned back and closed her eyes. "It's just sore there." He dug in again, using his thumbs, and she made no move to pull away this time. The look of relief and enjoyment on her face caused the blood flow to increase in several of his body parts—without the benefit of massage. He focused his thoughts back to her feet.

The problem was, her foot connected to her ankle, which he rubbed, and then to her calf, which he would rub next, and then to her thigh. His mind made the leap before his fingers got past her ankle, and the image of sliding his hands upward, under the loose material of her skirt sent a shock wave straight to his groin.

He couldn't stop now though, he'd only massaged one foot. He had to do the other. He *wanted* to do the other...and much more.

9

WHEN MATT'S HANDS slid upward to massage her calf, Dee moaned, causing him to break out in a sweat. Leaning back with her eyes closed, her face illuminated by the setting sun, she was more than any mortal man could resist. He had to look away before he leaned forward and kissed her.

Clamping his jaw tight, he trained his attention on her other foot. Again, she protested, only slightly this time, then relaxed into the movement of his hands. Unable to get past the constriction in his throat, Matt remained silent, determined to get through this without making a fool of himself.

But then she sighed, and when he looked up, he saw she was watching him. Something had changed between them. A stab of pure heat tightened his belly.

He willed his hands to keep massaging her foot, but they weren't paying any attention. His body was responding to the soft, sleepy look in her eyes when his palms slid upward. His fingers revisited her ankles, squeezing lightly, then skimmed up the backs of her calves over skin he'd already warmed with his touch. When he reached the backs of her knees and slipped past to the smooth skin of her thighs, he was close enough to kiss her.

So he did.

And she kissed him back. Languidly arching toward him without taking her hands from the hood of the car. This was the sensual, trusting side of Dee he'd only glimpsed before.

All his thoughts were narrowed down to the taste of her soft sweet mouth. After the first tentative touch, she made that sound again, part sigh, part whimper. He delved deeper into the kiss, using his tongue to coax her to respond. She did, meeting his tongue with her own in a dance that didn't require music. That pretty much scattered his last reasonable thought.

Matt's hands, still on autopilot, slid around her bottom and pulled her closer, to the edge, to him. And that's when things got crazy.

Dee couldn't think, didn't want to. As Matt dragged her closer, she reached for him, entwining her arms around his neck. Nothing mattered beyond sinking into his kiss like a woman half-starved and completely wild. All she needed was Matt, his mouth, his hands. Him.

She could feel his sure touch, fingers pushing under her skirt, cradling her bottom. She wanted to get closer, to rub against him, to make him feel as reckless and crazy as she was feeling, but he held her away. In defiance she brought her knees up and slid her calves around him. When her knee bumped the gun strapped to his hip, he retreated from the kiss.

He looked like a man in pain.

"Dee," he said, trying to bring them back to sanity, she supposed. "Wait just a second."

But it wouldn't work, couldn't work, because the deep, breathless sound of his voice gave him away. They'd been dancing around this for days, with every look, every touch. Dee wasn't in the mood to walk away. Not now. She didn't believe Matt wanted to, either.

"Why?" she asked.

"We need to talk about this."

Dee pushed her fingers along the strong line of his jaw, then rubbed his lips lightly with her thumb. "I don't want to talk." If they talked, she'd have to remember that she didn't need to depend on one man, even for sex. She'd have to shut down the glorious rush of sensual energy flowing through her and regain control.

Just this once she wanted to be completely out of control, and she wanted Matt to take her there. In one smooth motion she plucked his hat from his head and set it on the roof of the car. Then she angled her hand around his neck and tugged him forward for another kiss, something she'd wanted to do since they'd first stood in the dark at the lake.

He hesitated for a heartbeat before complying with her request. This time the kiss was slow and wet and deep. Dee lost track of everything but the movement of his lips sliding over hers, offering, promising.

An aching cascade of response slid through her

limbs. She could hardly breathe. His hands tightened on her back and drew her into him. And she went, willingly, gladly, wrapping her arms and her legs around him.

She bumped his gun again.

He broke away from her momentarily, long enough to unbuckle his gun belt and remove it. After placing it on the roof of the car next to his hat, he faced her. His sun-dazzled, brown eyes held her immobile for several long seconds before he spoke.

"Come on, then," he said in a low coaxing tone, before moving between her thighs once more.

Dee almost laughed in pure, sweet abandon, but her mouth was busy, and his fingers were dragging the tail of her blouse free. Then his hands were on her, covering her breasts, working the catch of her bra. In the next shattering moment his palms cradled her bare breasts, and the sensation was so intense, she could hardly breathe.

Matt felt more than heard Dee's surprised, indrawn breath. He knew what she was feeling because the echo of the contact had sent a shock wave of slow-rolling heat down his back, settling in the hardest part of him. No time now to remember that she was a big-city career woman who'd be gone in a few days. He knew Dee would leave, but at this moment, nothing mattered but touching, and tasting her.

Her breasts were perfect, yet filling his hands with her softness made him ache to do more.

"Unbutton your blouse," he whispered, unwilling to release her, even for a moment.

She did the best she could, he supposed, but her hands were sluggish and he couldn't resist kissing her. So, in the end he had to help her with the last two buttons. Without words, he guided her backward until she was lying flat on the hood of the car. When he pushed the soft silky material away to reveal her breasts, his heart tried to hammer its way out of his chest.

She was every cowboy's wet dream, lying there gazing up at him with sleepy half-closed eyes. Her skin looked molten, tinted by the fiery western sky, her nipples hardened points begging for his mouth.

They didn't beg long.

She wrapped her legs around him as he bent over her. Restless fingers raked through his hair as he laved first one nipple, then the other, dividing his complete and demanding attention between her breasts and her mouth.

He couldn't wait much longer. Her long skirt was already hiked up to thigh level so it didn't take much effort to slide his hand underneath. Dee went breathlessly still as he pushed his fingers under her panties and tugged them down. The material was wet and everywhere he touched her, she was hot. She whimpered his name and twisted closer to his touch. He eased two fingers inside her and her back arched off the car.

Ready.

Some distant part of his mind knew he ought to

slow down, to be sure she was *sure*. But he was beyond listening. He pulled his fingers free, and in a few quick movements, stepped away to remove her panties, then unzipped his pants. Dragging her hips to meet his, he slid into her tight softness.

Dee was surprised when he entered her, not because she hadn't expected it or wanted it, but because it felt so incredibly good. A long time had passed since she'd been intimate with a man, and although at the time she'd enjoyed the sensation, it had never felt like this before. She'd never been able to let go before.

As Matt retreated only to push into her again, she couldn't keep still. She had to touch him, to bring him closer, deeper. She raised up from the hood and put her arms around him. The roughness of his shirt and the cold snaps on his pockets scrubbed against her breasts, increasing the level of sensation.

Things went from fast to furious. She could feel every muscle in his back and shoulders as he drove into her, again and again. She wanted to help, but her limbs were weighted down with sensation. She could only offer her body, for his pleasure and her own.

Dee couldn't stifle a low, bone-melting sound of satisfaction as Matt's deep, rhythmic strokes sent her over the edge into a pulse-stuttering climax. In two more strokes, he buried his face in the bend of her neck and followed her over.

Several moments later, Dee felt warmth on her

face and opened her eyes. The setting sun had sent out one last brilliant blast of light to illuminate the hills before falling below the horizon. Dee drew in a deep breath and closed her eyes again. The smooth, solid hood of the car was beneath her, and Matt's warm weight held her immobilized. She felt completed, whole, and very, very alive. It should have scared her to death— her loss of control, her feeling of rightness in Matt's arms. But she decided not to allow anything to intrude, not yet.

The distant call of a hawk brought Matt to his senses. He took stock of the situation. Sergeant Matthew Travis, decorated officer of the Texas Rangers, had just made love to Dee Cates on the hood of his car, like a teenager during a hormone rush. And he felt lower than a snake under a rock about it. An elated and sexually satisfied snake, but a snake nonetheless.

Damn.

He'd lost his mind along with his professional ethics. He figured he'd better find a way to apologize to Dee before she got down off the car and found a rock big enough to kill him. What in the world was he going to say?

He could feel her breathing underneath him, and one of her hands slowly traced a path up and down his spine. Otherwise, she was utterly still. He didn't want to move, but he had to.

"Are you okay?" he asked as he pushed up to balance his weight on his arms.

Dee smiled instead of answering. She looked a

good bit better than okay. With her tossed hair and that drowsy, satisfied look in her eyes, she made the perfect picture of a well-loved woman. And the idea that he'd put that contented warmth in her gaze made him begin to harden all over again.

He pulled away before she could notice. No more craziness, they had to talk.

First he had to get them decent. He rearranged himself and fastened his pants, then tugged her skirt down before leaning over her again. "Hmm?"

"I'm fine," she answered.

"You sure?"

She smiled that sleepy smile and used his arms to pull herself up. "Yes, I'm sure." She kissed him lightly. "But thanks for asking."

Matt decided he might as well go ahead and bite the bullet. They were moving way too fast and it was all his fault. "I didn't mean for things to…" He had to clear his throat. "I didn't plan to—"

"I know." She looked down to button her blouse.

Matt brushed her hands away and finished the task. It was the least he could do. "I'm sorry," he said.

He had her attention then. She stopped him with a questioning look. "Why should you be sorry? There were two of us here. Either one of us could have stopped what happened."

"But I'm responsible."

"Why, because you're the man?"

"No, because I'm me. I don't usually seduce women on the hood of my car."

"And I for one am glad to hear that."

He watched her expression, her eyes. She seemed to be taking the whole thing rather lightly. Something about her flippant answers didn't ring true.

He put his hands on her arms to get her complete attention. "Are you sure you're okay?"

"I'm sure." She smiled and touched his cheek before kissing him softly on the mouth. "Now, will you hand me my boots?"

Matt helped Dee put on her boots and lifted her down from the car hood. When her feet touched the ground, they were face-to-face, breath-to-breath for a moment. He wanted to kiss her again, but remembering how his self-control had just been scrambled, he settled on a safer choice. He put an arm around her and walked her to the passenger door of the car.

On the way back to the driver's side, he almost stepped on her discarded panties. He picked them up and in the process, noticed they were still slightly damp to the touch. Matt had to close his eyes and take a deep breath to fight the surge of genuine, body-tightening lust that shot through him before he could manage the simple task of rebuckling his gun belt and replacing his hat.

10

DEE MANAGED to hold on to her dazed composure until she was alone in her hotel room. Only then did the full impact of the "interesting" afternoon she'd spent with Matt Travis, aka the Lone Star Lover, settle in to disturb her contentment. She'd known he was dangerous—tall, dark and reckless—but she hadn't known exactly how dangerous until he'd handed over the panties which she'd so willingly surrendered to him.

He'd driven her back to her car, coerced a promise from her to have dinner with him and informed her he would pick her up at her hotel at eight—no more meeting in parking lots.

And, much to her own amazement, she'd agreed. How had Matt gotten past her defenses, all her "too busy for men" excuses? She'd been busy today, all right, busy with the Lone Star Lover.

Dee dropped her purse on the dresser, backed up until her knees hit the bed then fell backward like a puppet without strings.

He'd kissed her goodbye. Pulled her into his arms and kissed her in front of God and everybody in the parking lot of Los Amigos Tex-Mex Restaurant. And she'd let him. Being close enough for their clothes to brush in public had brought back memories of dancing with him.

Dancing. Now *that*, she realized, was where this whole thing had begun to get out of hand.

Dee drew in a deep calming breath. Lying there in the dim silence of her room, she searched her memory for the lyrics of the song, or the steps, or anything safer than dissecting what had just happened between her and Matt.

Trouble was, even when he was out of sight, she could still feel the cool, solid surface of the car hood against her back. Still feel the urgent heat of Matt's mouth, his hands and…his body.

He'd overwhelmed her. No, they'd overwhelmed each other. Mr. Dependable had a reckless, wild streak of heat, and Dee Cates, the counterfeit Mz. Right, had been burned up by it. Now she had to decide what to do.

Part of her wanted to relax and enjoy the chemistry. She knew where her life was headed. She'd been taking the Pill for safety because her career would always come first. She didn't need commitment, or guilt, or support from a partner. What's the worst that could happen? What harm would it do to have a fling with a handsome, eligible man like Matt?

The problem, she realized, was that the word *fling* probably didn't exist in Ranger Matt Travis's vocabulary. *What's the worst that could happen?* He'd told her he was waiting for the right woman. What if he decided that woman was her? Dee knew she could never be what he wanted—

no matter how urgently they'd *wanted* each other earlier. Just thinking about it brought a flush of warmth to her face.

To short-circuit that dangerous line of thought, she forced herself to get up and head for the shower. Chemistry or not, she wasn't going to get trapped into depending on someone the way her mother had. She'd already allowed Matt to get closer than most. She'd told herself it was because he'd offered to help her. But now she wasn't so sure. She had to slow things down on the physical side before Matt's goals for the future, and her own, collided.

Tonight, Dee promised herself as she unbuttoned the blouse Matt had helped button for her earlier, cooler heads would have to prevail. The next time she saw him, she'd make sure Matt understood she wasn't interested in being his Mz. Right.

DEE CATES was absolutely *not* his type, Matt reminded himself as he shoved the door of his car shut and headed for his own front door. So what if she had a face and a smile that could cause a man to lose his head, and legs that could start a barroom brawl? No matter how beautiful or how responsive, she'd made it clear that she had no place in her life for a man. And he'd better remember that, because he could easily get in way too deep.

Deep. He was already on his toes and up to his neck. The memory of the sighing sounds she'd made when he'd been inside her made his skin itch. He wanted to touch her again, anywhere, everywhere. Whether she was serious or not.

No use volunteering for another round with a career woman. He'd been knocked out by one before. Trouble was, Dee already had him punch-drunk with the feel of her, with the way the two of them fit together. He knew he wouldn't be able to stay away from her if she wanted him. He'd take whatever she would be willing to give. He just had to make sure his heart didn't get involved. Because he also knew she would leave him. And he'd have to let her go.

His mailbox was stuffed full of messages, and he could hear the phone ringing as he turned the key in the lock. Hell. It had probably been ringing all day again. He really wasn't in the mood to fend off any more potential brides. He was too preoccupied with thoughts of Dee. So when he picked up the receiver, he said brusquely, "Listen, if you're calling about the ad, the position has been filled." He started to slam the phone down when he heard a male voice on the other end.

"So, when's the weddin'?"

Matt recognized his brother Nathan's voice and swore under his breath. "Cut that out," he ordered. Nathan's laughter only raised his hackles. "Why did you tell Ma all that bull Hazard fed you? Whose side are you on?"

"Why, you know I always have your best interests at heart," Nathan answered, as insincere as one of those "all hat and no cow" politicians up in Austin.

"Yeah, I bet." Matt had to stop himself from overreacting. The whole thing was supposed to be a joke, after all. "So how are you gonna bail me out on Sunday? I don't want to get the family involved in this foolishness."

"What's the big deal? Just bring her over to Mama and Daddy's, let the women in the family check her out, eat and leave. Nobody expects you to marry her on the spot."

"Look, I'm not plannin' to marry her at all. And she—"

"You mean, Bill Hazard *lied* to me?" his brother replied in mock outrage.

Matt drew in a calming breath. "Bill would lie to Saint Peter if it fit in with one of his practical jokes."

Nathan's voice fell to a normal tone. "So you're not actually seeing this woman?"

Matt thought about that for a moment. He'd been seeing Dee, all right. Seeing, touching…lovin'. "Well, yes and no."

"What the heck does that mean?"

"It means, it's none of your damn business."

"Ouch, big brother. Okay, I won't ask. But what are you gonna do about Sunday? You know Ma won't take no for an answer—and let's not *even* talk about Daddy."

"I'll see what Dee thinks about it tonight. We're going to eat down on the River Walk."

"Well, good luck on convincing her. You don't

want to face Ma if you show up on Sunday alone."

"Oh, I'm not worried. Not after I tell her that you and Bill were pulling a joke on me. She'll be hangin' *your* hide on the fence."

After a moment, Nathan cleared his throat. "I may be comin' down with the stomach flu. Can't eat barbecue on a queasy stomach."

"I wouldn't try to lie your way out of this. You know how Ma feels about liars."

"Yeah, the same way she feels about rat droppin's—lower than the lowest." Nathan sighed. "All I ask is, let me know if you're bringin' her or not. You know that old sayin', forewarned is forearmed, or somethin' like that... Oh, and speakin' of old Bill and being forewarned. He told me that a bunch of those women from the party have staked out Hurly's bar and are waitin' for you to show up. Hell, every single guy in the county is headed in this direction. If I were you, big brother, I'd watch my back. You might end up in the middle of a brawl yet."

"Damn. If this thing gets any more out of hand, I may have to go on TV just to save my skin. I think we should both stick to the Boy Scout motto, Be Prepared, because I have a feeling we're all gonna be sorry we ever met Bill Hazard."

DEE FELT more like herself again. She'd showered and dressed in her newly cleaned business suit, partly as a defense against any further lapses, and partly to remind Matt that she was first and foremost an independent career woman.

He'd called her from the lobby at exactly five minutes to eight and offered to walk her down. She'd declined. She was perfectly capable of finding the elevator and meeting him downstairs. She thought she was prepared to see him again after the intimacy of the afternoon, but when the elevator doors opened and he stood on the other side waiting, every nerve under her business attire went haywire.

"'Evenin'," he said, touching his hat.

On the surface, he appeared so polite and innocent. The perfect Texas gentleman: tan Stetson, white shirt, dark pants, a jacket and a tie. But Dee's gaze locked on his eyes, and when he looked at her, there was nothing innocent in his expression.

She felt her own cheeks warm and made a show of smoothing her jacket and checking the security of the purse strap over her shoulder before stepping closer. She searched for her tried-and-true aloof attitude but it seemed to have gone on strike where Matt was concerned. One side of his mouth quirked up as if he knew he'd gotten to her. Then, faster than bats could blink, he transformed into a gentleman again.

"You look very nice tonight," he said as he held out his arm.

"Thank you," she managed to say. At least when she had his arm, she didn't have to look into those mischievous brown eyes.

"How're your feet?"

Just hearing the question caused her to stumble. She vividly remembered where his earlier concern had taken them—several light-years past the point of no return. His arm tightened slightly to steady her and when she met his gaze, he was smiling.

"They're fine, why?" She knew her voice sounded breathless. She braced herself for his answer.

"I thought we'd eat at one of the restaurants on the River Walk but it's about three blocks from here." He looked down at the heels she'd had trouble with at the lake that first night. "Would you rather drive than walk?"

Relief coursed through Dee. Matt wasn't being obnoxious, snidely reminding her about her complete surrender. He was merely being courteous. She shrugged away her uneasy thoughts and returned his smile. "Believe it or not, I wear this type of shoe most of the time. I'm used to them. As long as there are no rocks between here and the restaurant, I'll be fine."

He tugged her forward. "Let's go, then. I'm starved."

Even though he'd said he wanted to hurry, he took his time. They strolled along the shops downtown filled with Indian art, jewelry, books and souvenirs like T-shirts printed with Don't Mess with Texas displayed for the steady flow of tourists who visited San Antonio every year.

As they turned another corner that would lead

them to the river, Matt asked, "Have you been to the Alamo?"

"No, actually I've been too—"

"Busy," he finished the sentence, then had the nerve to laugh at her look of outrage. She tried to pull her arm free to get a good angle for retaliation but he held on. "Okay, don't get riled," he soothed. "At least this time I can claim that you've been *busy* with me."

Her earlier thoughts haunted her. She'd been "busy," all right. Again, words failed her when the memory of what they'd been busy doing danced across her mind in full, sensual force. Luckily, they reached the bridge before she had to reply.

"Watch your step," Matt warned.

Dee needed to take his advice in more ways than one. She forced herself to concentrate on the stairs rather than think of Matt's hands and his mouth, and the hood of his car. *God, what would she have done if he'd walked her to his car?* Three more steps to the bottom. She made herself count them. One. Two. Three.

It was like entering a different city. "I'd forgotten how pretty this is," Dee said, admiring the old-world feeling of the place.

Built below street level, the River Walk cut through the center of downtown San Antonio. Sidewalks bordered the water on both sides and each bend of the river brought new restaurants, shops for local artists to sell their work and even an amphitheater built into the bank. A unique cultural center, the River Walk provided entertainment, food and shopping for tourists and residents alike.

"Let's go this way," Matt suggested. "There's a place I think you'll like."

Even though Thursday was technically a weeknight, the sidewalks were crowded with people. And the river was busy with open tour boats full of tourists. As they walked, several different types of music reached them from open verandas—from Mexican cantinas to Irish pubs. Matt pointed out interesting sights while Dee admired the lights, the color and the pure energy of the place.

By the time they reached the establishment Matt had chosen, Dee was starving. There was a line waiting to enter Emilio's, the upscale restaurant whose menu board boasted "the best steaks in Texas." Dee followed Matt to the maître d', resigning herself to a long wait.

"Ranger Travis, it's good to see you again," the maître d' said. "We'll have a table on the veranda in about fifteen minutes. Why don't you and the lady take a seat at the bar and I'll come to get you when it's ready."

Matt thanked him, and before Dee knew it, she was seated at the bar with a frozen margarita in front of her.

She raised her glass toward Matt in a toast. "Well, I'm impressed. You must either own stock in the restaurant or eat here regularly."

Matt's uncomfortable expression surprised Dee.

"Actually, I helped out a member of the owner's family once a couple of years ago. He insists that I eat here whenever I'm on the Walk."

"Sounds like a good deal."

"There's no deal. I pay for my meals. He just makes sure I can get a table, that's all." He sounded a little defensive.

"I didn't mean to imply anything," she said quickly. "What did you do for his family?" When he simply looked at her, she caught on. "Don't worry, I'm not taping the conversation."

Matt shrugged as if the favor wasn't worth mentioning. "It was one of those cases that fall through the cracks," he told her. "One of the owner's sons-in-law had been shot and the local police went through all the motions but didn't come up with any leads. So, after a year, the case was filed, unsolved. They came to me as a last resort."

"And you solved it?"

After taking a sip of his drink, he placed it back on the bar. "I turned up a witness that had been overlooked, reopened the case and worked with the local police to arrest the perpetrator."

"I'm impressed."

"Don't be. Like I told the Gonzales family, I don't have a magic wand. It all comes down to step-by-step police work. The difference is, I have more time than the local police to dig around.

When I take a case, I can stay on it until it pans out."

Dee couldn't help wondering how long he could help her with her father's case. How much time they had together before—

The maître d' approached them through the surrounding crowd. "Ranger Travis, we have your table now." He nodded to Dee. "If you will follow me."

AFTER THEY WERE seated and had ordered steak, of course, Matt did his best to change the subject. He didn't want to discuss his job with Dee. He had too many other things on his mind where she was concerned.

He'd been on edge since she'd walked out of the elevator looking so cool and unapproachable. Touching her had been torture because he'd wanted more. Every time she'd smiled, he'd wanted to pull her close and taste her mouth. And when she'd gracefully taken a seat at the bar and crossed those incredible legs, Matt had felt as if he might be having a heart attack.

Now they were cozily seated at a corner table on the veranda overlooking the River Walk. The fluctuating noise level around them would keep anyone from overhearing their conversation. So, as Dee took a sip of her margarita and looked at him, he spit the words out. "We need to talk."

She raised her eyebrows slightly. "About?"

Her calmness made him grit his teeth. Where was the hot, sensual woman he'd made love to earlier that day? He held her gaze so she'd know he was serious. "About this afternoon."

"Oh." She blinked and looked away. "Well, I don't really know what to say..." Her voice trailed off.

He reached across the table and covered her hand with his. "You could say whether you're happy about it, or whether you want to borrow my gun to shoot me."

She looked at him and a sweet smile curved her mouth. "I have no intention of shooting you," she answered. "It was just one of those things."

Matt wanted to keep her talking. "Does 'one of those things' happen often?"

Her smile wavered but she didn't look insulted. "Well, no, actually. It hasn't happened in quite a while."

Matt tightened his fingers over hers and couldn't stop his grin. "Can't say I'm sorry to hear that."

"How about you?" she asked.

"Well, now, I don't recall that particular thing ever happening to me before—on the car and all. I'm still not sure it wasn't a dream."

Dee's skin had gone rosy, and suddenly he knew she wasn't as unaffected as she was acting. He felt parts of his own body warm in response. The noise around them became an indistinct buzzing in his ears as he turned her hand over and put his, palm to palm, with hers. "I guess we both just went crazy there for a while."

She nodded but didn't speak. Matt sat there

looking into her amazing blue eyes, wanting to pull her into his arms again. To touch that rosy blush on her skin with his mouth. He had to rein himself in before he dragged her out of the restaurant.

"So, back to my original question. How do you feel about it?"

Her palm arched up to meet his briefly. "To be honest, I'm a little shell-shocked."

It was his turn to nod. "That's understandable."

"But you're right," she continued. "We do need to talk. I don't want you to get the wrong idea."

"And what idea might that be?" he asked, unable to stifle a smile.

"That having— I mean, making—" She frowned, drew in a breath and said, "What we did this afternoon doesn't mean anything."

Matt's smile faltered. "You're gonna have to explain that statement to me, because from where I sit, things look a little different."

"I didn't intend that the way it sounded." She pulled her hand from beneath his and reached for her drink. Matt noticed that her hand shook slightly as she raised it to her mouth. After taking a sip, she explained. "We had a deal. You'd help me investigate my father's disappearance and I'd pretend to be your Mz.— Your date."

Matt nodded, unwilling to interrupt.

"We just got a little carried away," she added.

"I think at this point we should remember our original purpose."

"And that would be?"

She placed her hand on his this time. He couldn't tell whether it was to emphasize her point or to comfort him. "No matter what happened between us, you need to remember I'm only playing a part."

Matt kept his features perfectly blank. He'd known when she started talking what she was about to say. No surprise. But that didn't mean he had to like it worth a damn. *Keep it light, son, or she'll run like a rabbit.* And he wasn't ready to let her go just yet. Whatever else happened after this, he wasn't about to set her off by going all possessive on her. He could play any game as long as he knew the rules. Especially this particular game with this particular woman.

He offered her his best "cowboy" grin. "Why, Mz. Cates, you're jumpin' the gun a little bit there, aren't you? You haven't even seen my scar yet."

Matt watched her react first to his smile and then to the words. The smooth, pale peach color of her face warmed by a few shades. When he'd let her squirm enough, he squeezed her hand. "Don't worry. I remember the deal. I just wanted to know whether you enjoyed our afternoon together."

Dee drew in a long, slow breath then leveled her gaze on his. "I think you know I did."

"Then let's not spoil it with overanalyzing. I'm a man, you're a woman. What happened this afternoon proved that. Why don't we just let it go and see what happens?"

11

SEE WHAT HAPPENS… Dee felt a quiver of anticipation. Could she let go? Let nature take its course, so to speak? Every time she and Matt were within ten feet of each other, the spark of attraction between them grew hotter, more insistent. She didn't want to be the one to figuratively throw a bucket of water on it. She wanted to step a little closer and enjoy the heat.

Sitting up a little straighter, Dee said, "You're right. After all, we're both consenting adults. As long as we're honest with each other, why squelch the natural chemistry?"

Matt's mouth softened and he nodded in agreement. "Sounds like a plan."

The warm, smoky look in his eyes made Dee nervous again. She had to set the record straight. "All we have to remember is that you aren't really the Lone Star Lover, and I'm not your Mz. Right."

"Well, now, I seem to remember some things about this afternoon that had to do with lovin' and felt pretty right," he said, unfazed.

If charm could be aimed, she'd just taken a direct hit. Dee gathered her defenses to refute his words but he beat her to the punch line.

With a laugh, he raised a hand. "Don't worry. I

know what you're sayin'. I just want you to know that if there are any other chemistry experiments you feel the need to conduct, I'm willin'.''

By silent assent, they spent the rest of their meal chatting about the food and her dad's case. They also did a fair amount of people watching. As the parade of tourists and conventioneers passed by on the Walk below them, they alternately chose a couple and made up a history for them—the military honeymooners from Oklahoma, the East Coast condo couple, the future dentists of America from Ohio.

As they left the restaurant, Dee was still smiling over Matt's last designation of a young couple with four children in tow as ''the couple voted most likely to create their own Little League baseball team.''

It seemed natural for Matt to put his arm around her and rest his hand on her back as they walked. And even though there were several layers of cloth between his palm and her skin, she could feel the heat of his touch. When they strolled under the shadow of one of the many bridges over the river, it seemed perfectly reasonable for Matt to pull her close and kiss her.

His hands casually brushed up the sleeves of her jacket as his mouth touched hers, but there was nothing casual about the slow, tongue-dancing kiss they shared. Just as Dee stepped closer for more contact, she heard a voice behind her.

"Well, is that Matthew Travis?" a man said, louder than Dee thought necessary.

Matt kept her still with his hands, but he ended the kiss and looked over her shoulder. She heard him swear under his breath before turning her toward the sound.

"Bill. Fancy meetin' you here," Matt said, but his voice sounded tight. He touched the brim of his hat and added, "Rayanne." He turned to Dee. "Dee Cates, this is my *friend*, Bill Hazard. You met him the other night. And his wife, Rayanne."

Dee couldn't help noticing the emphasis he put on the word *friend*. Then, slightly embarrassed at being caught in such a private moment, she did her best to be polite. Bill nodded to her and she shook Rayanne's hand. The woman studied her with an unmistakable mischievous grin. She and her husband were obviously enjoying Matt's discomfort.

"I don't suppose you've talked to my brother Nathan lately?" Matt asked.

Bill rubbed his chin as if the question required deep thought. "Now, I do talk to him from time to time." He turned to his wife. "Did I mention speaking to Nathan today?" he asked innocently.

"I'm not sure," she said, and matched his tone.

"The next time you talk to him," Matt nearly growled, "tell him he's a dead man."

Dee looked back and forth between the men, trying to figure out what they were really saying. Rayanne stepped into the lull of conversation. "I hear you work for a television station in Austin," she said. "That must be exciting."

"Yes, it is," Dee replied truthfully. "I love my job."

"How are you two going to work that out after you're married?" Rayanne asked.

Matt's arm tightened around her briefly. *Remember the deal*, Dee reminded herself. "Well, I'm checking into a position at our affiliate here in San Antonio."

Apparently satisfied with Dee's answer, Rayanne nodded. "That should work out fine, then." She glanced at her husband then back to Dee. "I hear you'll be meeting Matt's whole family this Sunday."

Dee heard Matt say something under his breath as she turned to him. "I will?" she asked, unable to elaborate on a topic she hadn't heard a word about.

"Uh, yes. You remember, I mentioned my mom called and invited us out to the ranch for a barbecue." His gaze asked her to go along with his leading statement.

She hesitated long enough for him to get firmly out on the lonely limb he'd chosen. "Oh, that's right," she added finally. "I didn't know that I would be meeting the whole family though."

"Ha. Wild horses couldn't keep them away," Bill answered. "Once they found out old Matthew here had found the woman of his dreams, they just had to plan a get-together to meet you."

Matt was conspicuously silent. Dee intended to

have a long talk with him about this later, but right now she wasn't going to give Bill and his wife any more information than necessary.

"I'm sure that'll be fun," she said.

Without further ammunition, Bill glanced at his watch. "You two eat yet?" he asked.

"Yes, at Emilio's," Matt answered. "You should try it." It sounded more like an order than a suggestion.

"A little too pricy for us regular Department of Safety employees," Bill said. "We'll settle for a beer and some nachos. You know I put Johnny and Tom in charge of the leftover women from your little party. I'm sure we'll bump into them around here somewhere. If you two want to come along, I'll buy you a beer."

Both Dee and Matt said, "No, thank you," at the same time.

Dee could feel a blush on the way. When Matt looked down at her, she stammered her excuse. "I have an early day tomorrow—working on a story. I need to turn in pretty soon." The blush blossomed full force as the meaning of her words sunk in. She sounded as if she couldn't wait to get Matt into bed. This was getting worse by the minute.

Bill laughed and swatted Matt's shoulder. "I can see you two want to be alone. Don't blame you a bit. Nice to meet you, Ms. Cates." After they said their goodbyes, Bill tugged Rayanne back in the opposite direction. Whatever he said after that was out of their hearing. Dee did, however, catch the sound of him laughing heartily at some private joke between him and his wife.

Matt stood staring at their backs as they walked away. "Well, in case we weren't before, we're now officially engaged," he said. Dee couldn't tell if he was happy about that, or ready to commit murder. "Come on." He coaxed her toward the stairs. "Let's get out of here before my brother shows up."

Dee wasn't budging just yet. "When were you going to tell me about this party on Sunday?"

Matt lifted his hat and ran a hand through his hair before resettling the Stetson. "I was hoping to get out of it."

"Out of telling me, or out of the party?"

He cocked his hands on his hips. "Both, but mostly out of taking you to my parents'."

"What's the matter? Afraid they won't approve of me?"

Matt looked speechless. Dee had no idea why she'd said what she did, but it probably had more to do with payback than teasing. She was beginning to feel like a bug under a microscope in a world full of eyes—watching. And, truth be told, spending time with the reckless Lone Star Lover felt safer than getting to know Mr. Dependable and his whole family.

"Approval has nothing to do with it. I don't like the idea of gettin' my family involved in something started by a joke. And I really don't like being forced to lie."

"So, why don't we go out there on Sunday and

tell them the truth? That you've been helping me with an investigation and that I have to be back at work on Monday. Case closed."

Matt shook his head sadly. "You don't know my family." Suddenly, he scanned the people around them warily. "One on one, they're not too bad. But you get 'em in a bunch and you've got trouble. Speaking of family, I wasn't kidding when I said my brother might show up. He's the only one who knew we'd be on the Walk tonight. He obviously told Bill." He took her arm again. "Let's go and talk about this somewhere else."

BY THE TIME they made it back to the lobby of Dee's hotel, Matt had reacquired his sense of humor about the whole thing. But it still rankled him that whatever happened between him and Dee was based on one of Bill's practical jokes. He didn't see anything funny about how he felt, or how she felt in his arms.

And he didn't want to discuss dinner with his family any further. He'd already dodged enough bullets for one night. He remembered how she'd blushed when she'd said she had to turn in early and decided a little teasing was in order.

"What's this big story you're working on early in the morning?" he asked. "You haven't been thumbin' through that *Texas Men Magazine* again, have you?"

Dee elbowed him lightly in the ribs. "Very funny, Lone Star. And just when have I had time to interview other men?" She turned and smiled up at him.

"Who knows what you do after business hours?" He gazed into her sparkling blue eyes. "I know if you called me in the middle of the night, I'd tell you anything." He hoped his grin offset the truth of those words. No use letting her know he'd thought about her several times when he should have been sleeping.

"Anything, huh?" she replied. Her sultry expression made his pulse leap.

"Excuse me," a bellman said, wanting them to either go into the lobby or get out of the doorway.

Matt took Dee's arm and guided her toward the elevators. "Come on. I'll ride up with you."

"You really don't have to…"

He gave her his best bad-cop look and pushed the button at the bank of elevators. "No problem at all, ma'am."

"Oh, pleeeeese. If you call me ma'am ever again I'll consider it an act of war," Dee threatened in mock outrage as she stepped into the empty elevator and pushed the button for her floor.

Matt let the doors close behind him. Then he kept moving forward, crowding Dee until her back was pressed against the mirrored wall. He braced a hand on either side of her head to convince her to stay put. "What was it the hippies used to say about war?"

Dee seemed a little out of breath and her gaze had gone all smoky and soft. "I believe it was something about making love," she whispered. But his kiss interrupted her. And she let it. Hell, she helped. By the time the elevator doors opened on the eighth floor, she had her hands inside his jacket.

She gave him a little push in the direction of the doors. Without words they walked arm in arm down the hall. And when they reached her door, she handed him her key. Like the gentleman his mama had taught him to be, he hesitated after opening the door. Everything he wanted was waiting for him on the other side. All he had to do was follow.

"Are you sure?" he asked.

"I'm sure," she answered. "Besides, it's time I got a good look at that scar."

Dee knew she'd danced into dangerous territory once more. Being alone with Matt "Tall, Dark and Reckless" Travis should have worried her. But it didn't. She wanted to let his heat flow over her again, to welcome it. To see if the combination would still be as inflammatory as it had been that afternoon.

She shouldn't have doubted it. As soon as he touched her, running his palms along her silk blouse and up her back, she knew everything would be just as hot.

She shoved his jacket off his shoulders and started on his tie as he removed his hat and tossed it on the night table. His mouth seemed to gain momentum after reluctantly moving from her lips to her ear, to her neck. As he unbuttoned her blouse, he touched each exposed section of skin with his lips…and his tongue.

Dee lost all thought and her hands moved clumsily. Finally, he dragged his tie loose and slipped it over his head. Soon the rest of their clothes were scattered, his boots draped with her panty hose, and they were tumbling on clean white sheets.

Matt paused with his mouth millimeters from hers and his fingers inches from the aching tightness of her nipples. Dee tried to stay on track. Her chest was too constricted to speak normally, so she whispered, "Show me your scar."

"Later," he said, his lips transmitting the sound directly into her mouth.

The natural chemistry between them exploded once more and Dee felt she couldn't touch him fast enough, couldn't urge him close enough. When he paused after a particularly scintillating escapade involving his tongue and several quivering parts of her anatomy, she couldn't hide her impatience. "Please," she pleaded. She didn't care about the past, the future, the *deal*. She wanted him inside her. Now.

"Dee?" His voice sounded as strained as her patience.

She couldn't form words. Sounds would have to do. "Hmm?"

"The last time—" he paused to swallow and take a breath "—I, we didn't use any protection and I…"

"It's okay, I'm on the Pill," she answered, then tried to drag his mouth down to hers.

She'd almost accomplished her mission when he added, "I just want you to know you're safe with me."

Then he was kissing her and the logical part of her mind turned the words over and over while the rest of her reveled in his complete physical attention. She'd known she was safe with him, even as he'd recklessly made love to her on the hood of his car. That damn dependable part—

"Oh," she breathed as he entered her in one slow, smooth push. "Oh," she said again as Matt's heat melded with her own. Nothing mattered but the shivery pleasure of each touch, each stroke. "Oh, Matt…yes."

TWO HOURS LATER, they lay tangled in the sheets. Matt's face was pressed into the pillow but his arm was flung across her belly. Dee opened her eyes, feeling boneless and satiated. She needed to make a trip to the bathroom, but she didn't want to move just yet. She made a desultory study of the unfamiliar ceiling of her hotel room. Funny, she hadn't noticed that reflection of red light before. She turned her head slightly to find the source—the message light on her phone. She hadn't seen it when they'd come in, but then, she'd had other things on her mind.

Dee kissed Matt's arm then turned under its weight to reach the phone. Matt stirred and shifted over onto his back.

"Did you notice the phone ringing?" she asked, although she wasn't serious. Surely they couldn't have missed the phone. Out of reflex she wet her lips...she could still taste him. Maybe they *had* missed the phone, she decided.

Matt propped an extra pillow under his head and smiled. "Well, I heard something but it was more like a tornado or a freight train." He ran teasing fingers along her ribs and lightly brushed her breast. "I heard another sound, too. A feminine sort of growl..." He made the male equivalent and Dee almost dropped the receiver.

"Hush," she admonished, but she could already feel her body responding to the sound, to his touch...again. Determined, she pushed the button for retrieving messages and waited.

Her boss's voice came over the line. "Dee. Call me as soon as you get in—no matter what time. We need your help."

"Damn," she said under her breath, not realizing she'd said it out loud.

Matt stopped his playful exploration. "What's wrong?"

Dee sat up and pulled the edge of the sheet around her. She rummaged through the clothes on the floor, settling on Matt's shirt. As she slipped it on, she explained, "That was my boss. I've got to call him back." She stood and headed to the bathroom. First things first.

Matt had pulled on his slacks by the time she returned. He sat on the edge of the bed and waited while she dialed the call.

"Who's the 'we' I'm supposed to help?" she asked when Jim answered the phone.

"Good evening to you, too," he said.

"Uh-huh. What's up?"

"Sorry to bother you on your vacation, but we have a small emergency. You know Richard is supposed to emcee the Community Service Awards Saturday night?"

"Yes, and…"

"He's got the flu, big-time. Can't speak without coughing. His doctor says it'll be at least three or four days before he can even do the news. We can cover him on the air, but we need someone to step in for the awards dinner. Here's your big chance, kid."

Dee had little doubt that Jim was telling the truth about Richard. Being the anchorman was Richard Reardon's life. She knew he would never pass up an opportunity for some personal PR like doing the awards banquet. And Jim knew she'd never pass it up either. Careerwise, this could only help her.

"He must be critical," she replied caustically. Then she realized exactly what taking Richard's place would mean. Her exhilaration slipping a few notches, she ran a hand through her hair and looked at Matt. It would mean going back to Austin on Saturday. Instead of having three more days to be with him, she'd only have two.

She let out a breath. She couldn't be in two places at once, and she needed to be in Austin Saturday night. "Where am I going, and what time do I have to be there?"

"Thanks, Dee. I owe you big-time for this, not to mention Richard. Come to think of it, missing it will probably be punishment enough for him. Rehearsal at the Driskoll Hotel at five. Banquet starts at seven. You know the drill, wear your sequins."

Matt watched Dee hang up the phone and knew she was about to say something he didn't want to hear.

"It looks like I have to leave earlier than I'd planned," she said.

Yep, Matt thought, something he definitely didn't want to hear. Five minutes ago she'd been in his arms. Two minutes ago he'd been enjoying the fact that his shirt looked better on her than it had ever looked on him. Now, after one simple phone call she seemed as distant and unapproachable as she had the first night they'd met. "What's going on?"

She scooted toward the headboard, picked up a pillow and stuffed it behind her back for comfort before speaking. "I have to go back to Austin and fill in for the emcee of the Community Service Awards banquet. The station sponsors the event every year along with the governor's office. Our anchorman usually handles the job but he has the flu."

"When?"

"Saturday night."

Saturday night. Matt couldn't think of a damn

thing to say. He'd known all along she couldn't stay forever, but he'd filed that information so far back in his mind the actual words took him by surprise. *Saturday night—day after tomorrow.* Dee looked as stunned as he felt.

"What are we going to do about the investigation?" she asked, then stopped. Her eyes widened. "What are you going to tell your family when I don't show up on Sunday?"

Matt held up a hand to stop her. "Whoa, one thing at a time." He'd known her job would take her away sooner or later, she'd made that clear. Seemed as though it was going to be sooner.

But right now he had to touch her. Time was running out on the opportunity to have her within reach. Instead of moving to the head of the bed and pulling her into his arms the way he wanted, he simply put a hand on her ankle. "How long will the banquet take?"

Dee sighed. "I have to be there at five but I'll need to go back to my place earlier to get dressed and do my hair. My part of the event officially ends with the ten o'clock news segment, but it wouldn't hurt to stick around and schmooze. In my business, public relations is important."

"I'm sure it is," Matt agreed. "Well, I had planned to trailer the horses out to the lake tomorrow to cover the rest of the area we found. I talked that buddy of mine who does aerial photography for surveyors into flying over that part of the county and taking a look. He said he saw a couple of old mining shacks out there. It's worth investigating, but it'll take most of a day. I could do that without you—" he shot her a smirk "—but I was sort of lookin' forward to seeing how well you ride."

His teasing didn't have much of an effect on her serious mood.

"I'm sorry, but this is my job. I can't say no."

"Hey, I'm not asking you to. If anyone can understand duty coming before pleasure, it's me." He squeezed her ankle to accent his words. "How about this? Austin isn't that far away. How about if we take the horses out tomorrow, then you could go home Saturday morning. I could drive up to Austin early Sunday morning and bring you back down here—" he ran his hand up her shin to her knee, "—so you can keep my family from lynchin' me."

Dee watched him for a moment. He could see her mind working. "There's no need for you to drive all the way to Austin," she said.

"Won't bother me a bit. I spend most of my time on the road." He paused, then decided to tell as much of the truth as he'd admit to. "I'm not ready to let you go yet."

Dee almost agreed. She didn't want to go...yet, but she also didn't want Matt to get the idea that her job wasn't important to her. She'd already allowed him to practically take over her whole life.

Her life.

The thought of her life without Matt Travis in it made her heart ache. But even though she didn't want to give him up yet, she couldn't pretend to be someone she wasn't just because she would miss him. They'd both known from the beginning that this relationship was temporary. Moments later, an idea began to take form, a way to show him once and for all, no matter how much chemistry had been stirred up between them, she couldn't be his real-life Mz. Right.

She decided to take him to Austin with her.

12

THE NEXT MORNING, Matt insisted on driving. So, after a stop for coffee and an abbreviated breakfast, they were headed north. The sun was barely above the horizon, and even after having two cups of coffee, Dee's eyelids looked heavy.

He'd enjoyed last night—maybe too much. He still didn't understand how he'd gotten roped into attending a highfalutin governor's award banquet, though. It wasn't his idea of a good time.

The conversation had gone something like: *Well, if you can lead me on a hike and a trail ride over the south forty acres of nowhere, then you can certainly put on a tux and eat dinner while I work.*

The only part that made the trip to Austin worthwhile was not having to say goodbye to Dee just yet. When she'd ushered him out of her room at about three in the morning, he'd been reluctant to leave. Having sex was one thing, but sleeping together constituted a whole different level of intimacy. A level he could tell Dee wasn't ready to share. But he would have traded several nights' sleep for the opportunity to hold her in his arms the whole night through.

Hell. The situation had climbed way beyond the high-water mark. He had to keep reminding himself that after this weekend Dee would disappear out of his life. What was between them had to do with their deal—then they'd go their separate ways.

Separate ways.

Unless he could convince her otherwise. The fledgling hope that he could find a way to keep her close had sprung up in his heart like a flower in the desert. But he had no brilliant plan to make that hope a reality. Until he did, he couldn't think about beginnings or endings. The future would have to chart its own course. He could only enjoy the present.

He glanced at Dee. It was apparent she wasn't much of a talker in the morning. She had her head back and her eyes half-closed watching the miles slide by in silence.

"You awake yet, sleepyhead?" he asked, then tried to look harmless so she wouldn't hit him.

Dee could feel the warmth of his sexy, "aw shucks" grin across the few feet of air separating them. And the pure power it wielded over her senses scared her to death. If he could make her body react without even touching, what else might he be able to do? He couldn't make her love him, could he?

Wide-awake now and worried, Dee found she couldn't speak, so she merely nodded her head. Matt didn't seem fazed by her silence.

"My brother said he'd bring the horses up and leave them in the pen by the barn," Matt said as he drove. "We'll trailer them out to the lake from there. Are you sure you're up to this?"

"Yeah." She cleared her throat and tried to regain her inner footing. "I'm even dressed properly for the occasion." She ran a hand along her khaki-covered thigh. *Wouldn't miss it for the world*, her mind taunted. For once, she admitted to herself that her determination had little to do with finding out about her father, and a lot to do with the man sitting next to her.

She turned her head to look out the window again. Moisture stung her eyes and her chest felt tight. She couldn't allow him to derail her life. Love or no love. She wasn't the type to quietly sit at home and make lemonade while her man went out to track down hardened criminals. She loved her job too much. And her job required most of her waking hours at this point.

No. This was the last day she would spend with Matt searching for information about her father. She needed to keep her mind on the goal and try not to think about how to say goodbye.

MATT GUIDED his horse to the top of the ridge and looked out over the shallow streambed on the other side. They'd arrived at the stacked pile of rocks he'd previously found, the same place where they'd turned back before, when they'd been on foot.

The memory of that day and the effect of rubbing her aching feet shot through him like a lightning bolt. He had to unobtrusively adjust his seat in the saddle because his jeans suddenly felt too tight. *Keep your attention on the business at hand*, he warned his wayward mind. Then he glanced behind him to check Dee's progress.

True to her word, she'd proved she could ride. She'd even helped him tack up, and strapped their lunch bundle on the back of her saddle with only one broken fingernail to show for it. He hadn't convinced her to wear a hat, though. She'd given him some female mumbo jumbo about wearing sunscreen. He looked up at the sun shining brilliantly in the cloudless blue sky. No need to worry, the worst heat of the summer was past. The cool, clear air of the foothills would keep her from roasting, and the horse he'd put her on, Buddy, was unlikely to dump her and light out for his pasture.

"How are you doin' back there?" he called.

"Just fine," Dee answered. "Isn't this the place we were before?" she asked.

"Yep. Once we pass the marker, we need to keep our eyes open for any signs of life. Do you need to stop for anything?"

"No, let's keep going."

Matt pulled a plastic bottle of water out of his saddlebag and unscrewed the top. When Dee was close enough to bump knees with him, he offered her the bottle.

"This is a lot better than hiking it," Matt said.

Dee swallowed some of the water and nodded her head. "Yeah, but I have the feeling my backside is going to regret this tomorrow." She handed the bottle back to Matt and leaned forward to talk to her horse. "No offense, Buddy, but you could go on a diet. You are way too round."

Matt chuckled, but had to fight the sudden image produced by the fantasies in his brain—*starring him*, rubbing Dee's saddle-sore backside. He used all his concentration to close the water bottle and slide it back in place.

"Let's move on, then, before you hurt Buddy's feelings. He might find out you've got our lunch balanced on his back and toss you in the dust."

They rode slowly for the next two hours, checking every deer trail and switchback they came across. The ground in front of them grew rockier and several times they had to dismount and lead the horses up steep, unstable inclines.

Breathing in a lungful of evergreen-scented air mixed with dust, Matt decided that this was where he belonged. He should have been born a hundred or so years ago. He'd always felt better out in the open, rain or shine. The rugged terrain suited him just fine. He enjoyed depending on the surefooted step of a well-trained horse accompanied by the creaking sounds of his well-worn saddle leather and the faraway cries of a hungry hawk. Inwardly smiling at his romantic Old West notions, Matt was about ready to change directions when he spotted a grayish-red rag tied to a bush.

He pulled up and got down to investigate. Dee followed suit.

"What is it?" she asked.

"Just an old faded bandanna, but it didn't get here by accident. Somebody tied it as a marker." Matt walked around the immediate area while Dee held the horses. He finally found what he'd been looking for—a footprint. After studying the mark that might have been made by a boot heel, Matt looked from the ground to the bright, cloudless sky. The last rain he remembered had been the week before, so that meant the print was recent enough to be useful.

The direction of the footprint led off down a faint trail. Whoever had left the boot mark didn't come this way very often. Matt stood, dusted off his hands and walked back to Dee and the horses.

"Somebody's been here not too long ago. Let's see where he went."

They remounted, and with Matt in the lead they coaxed the horses through the trees and bushes. Twenty minutes later they maneuvered their way up a low hill. When they reached the top, Matt pointed off to the right.

Dee shaded her eyes and looked. It was a cabin. Well, sort of a cabin. You could see daylight through the walls and part of the tin roof was bent and hanging off one side. She couldn't imagine anyone living in it.

As they moved closer, Dee could see piles of different objects: rocks, tin cans, bicycle rims. The area was littered by what looked like small rock slides.

"It's an old mining site," Matt said. "We must

be getting close to the river. The place looks empty, but let's take it slow."

The horses picked their way through the scrub and the piles of junk until Matt put a hand up. He twisted in his saddle to face her.

"Stay on your horse," he ordered. "This is a perfect place for snakes." Then he swung a leg over and dismounted. Walking carefully around the different collections of rusty old refuse, he stepped up to the rickety door and gave it a push with his boot.

The door swung open on wobbly hinges.

Dee watched Matt lean one hand on the weathered wall and look inside before entering. Just then something small and dark ran from under several rotting boards near the cabin to one of the piles closer to the horses. Matt's horse snorted and backed into Buddy. Buddy sidestepped but held steady. Dee's hands tightened on the reins and her heart pounded in her chest. She didn't want to get to know any of the residents living in or under the shack.

She looked from pile to pile worrying that any minute a rattlesnake would rear its ugly head. What in the world was she doing out here? She belonged in the city, with concrete and skyscrapers and people, not out in the foothills playing Texas Ranger with Matt. Then a truly terrifying thought struck her. What if a rattlesnake bit Matt? She'd have to find a way to get help. The thought of him in pain or near death rocked her equilibrium. Suddenly, she couldn't stand the fact that he was out of her sight.

"Do you see anything?" Dee called, giving in to temporary panic. Her voice sounded two octaves higher than normal. She needed to hear his voice.

He didn't answer.

Dee was just psyching herself up to step down and brave a walk through the junky yard, rattlesnakes and all, when Matt reappeared. He had an empty tin can in his hand. He scanned the yard once more and took several slow steps toward the line of brush to the east.

"What is it?" Dee asked, trying not to harangue him for scaring her.

Matt picked up his horse's reins and walked over to her. Resting a hand on Buddy's neck, he held up the can for her to see.

"Chef Boyardee," he said. "Most of the label is still intact."

"What does that mean? Are we looking for an Italian?" Dee asked, unable to see the significance. Still skittish from worry, she kept a tight grip on Buddy's reins because she could feel her hands shaking.

Matt chuckled and tossed the can toward one of the piles. "No, it means someone has been living here recently. There are a few cooking pots and a platform covered with rags you could call a sleeping pallet."

He pushed his Stetson back and looked east. "Nobody around now, probably not for a week or so."

"So, what do we do now?"

"Well, I think we—"

"Hey!" A harsh, menacing voice accompanied by rustling bushes interrupted him. "Who are you? And what are you doin' sneakin' around my place?"

Matt raised his gaze to Dee and gave her a warning look before he turned in the direction of the raspy voice. He didn't need to tell her to be still and quiet—her heart had lodged in her throat a full thirty seconds before. Matt moved slowly, giving whoever was speaking a clear view of his hands, his gun belt and the polished single-star badge on his chest.

Dee squinted her eyes and searched the surrounding brush until she saw the owner of the voice. Something long and dark poked through the bushes at them. To Dee, it looked like the barrel of a rifle. She remembered Matt's scar and her mouth went completely dry.

"I'm Ranger Matt Travis, and this is Miss Dee Cates. We're lookin' for an old-timer who used to live out here. Went by the name of Tinker."

"A Ranger you say?" The bushes rustled again and a head poked through. The man wiped the sweat out of his eyes and studied them intently. "Hmmph." Seemingly satisfied by what he saw, he stepped out into the open. Dee realized that what she'd thought was a gun was actually a gnarled stick of mesquite, polished smooth like blood-red ivory. She pressed a hand over her heart and willed it to beat normally.

The man appeared as old and gnarled as his walking stick. His thin, gunmetal-gray hair was tied back in a ponytail. Another strip of cloth was tied around his forehead, revealing a weather-lined face that could have been anywhere from forty to ninety years old. The knuckles of his large hands were knobbly but the grip he had on the stick spoke of true strength.

As he shuffled closer, Dee took it as a good sign that her horse, Buddy, didn't seem afraid of him.

"What do you want with Tinker?" he asked. "He died years ago."

"You knew him?" Matt asked.

"You could say that." The man ambled to a halt five feet from them. He shaded his deep-set eyes with one hand and looked up at Dee. He studied her without any change in his forbidding expression. "Don't see many women out here. You're a pretty one, too."

"Thank you," Dee replied, her manners overriding the situation. What was she supposed to say to a man who looked as if he'd been living in a cave for thirty years?

He returned his gaze to Matt. "She your wife?" he asked.

Dee saw Matt's mouth twitch, but his face remained serious. "No, sir. She's a good friend."

"Well, I don't like people diggin' around my claim. If you want to know somethin', come out and ask me."

Matt touched the brim of his hat as a show of respect. "That's exactly what we'd like to do."

Dee started to dismount so that she could be included in the conversation, but the old man raised his stick defensively and she stopped.

"Just stay up there, miss. I don't like people snoopin'," he said again. "This is my land and this is my dig. If you want to talk, you come to my place by the river." With that he turned and headed back the way he'd come.

With a shrug to Dee, Matt, leading his own horse, fell into step behind the old man, leaving her and Buddy to bring up the rear.

MATT USED the walking time to calm down. He was furious—with himself. Bringing Dee out into the middle of nowhere and putting her in danger was unforgivable. On the surface it hadn't seemed dangerous, no more than a trail ride through the hills. But when he'd heard the old-timer yell and seen what looked like a gun, he realized how stupid he'd been. Although he'd die before he let anyone hurt her, this episode drove home the fact that Dee belonged in her safe world of banquets, interviews and the politically correct, not in his uncertain environment of guns, criminals and danger.

After following a barely discernible trail for fifteen or twenty minutes, Matt could smell the musty, damp odor of the river. The aroma reminded him of the hundreds of times he'd gone fishing with his dad and brothers. The ground flattened out and soon they could see the sparkle of moving water. The old man led them to a run-down camper-trailer with an outside fire pit and a muddy three-wheeled all-terrain vehicle parked in front.

Matt helped Dee down, then tied the horses close enough to drink from the river. The old man sat on a worn, split-back truck seat that had been bolted down to some two-by-fours next to an ancient car tire filled with dirt and flowers. Then he unenthusiastically motioned for them to sit on the log opposite him.

"Now," he huffed once they were seated. "What about old Tinker? You lookin' to put him in jail? He never did nothin' but mind his own business."

"No, sir. Nothin' like that," Matt assured him. "We wanted to ask him a few questions about a man who disappeared in this area around eighteen years ago."

"Disappeared, huh? And you think old Tinker killed him?"

Matt's instincts suddenly sharpened. Why would this man assume the man they were looking for was dead? "We don't know what happened," he said. "All we know is that the man—" he glanced at Dee, "—Dee's father, disappeared. We're trying to find someone who might have seen him."

"You sure ain't gonna find him out here now." He scrubbed a hand along his whiskered chin. "I haven't seen much of any living things, only deer, rabbits, snakes and a few fishermen." He pointed a knobbly finger at Dee. "Was your daddy a fisherman?"

Dee cleared the dust from her throat before she spoke. "Uh, no. He used to hunt for Indian relics, pottery and arrowheads."

The man's gaze focused on some distant point down the river. "Pottery, you say?"

"Yes, sir."

"I've collected some pottery over the years. You know, before Tinker passed on, he left me some things you might like to see. Want to?"

"Well, that's very nice of you..." Dee shot Matt a sideways glance. "But I really need to find information about my father. Do you think you can help us?"

He raised his stick in the direction of the horses. "You got any city food, like spaghetti, in those bags?"

"No, sir, no spaghetti. We have some ham and cheese sandwiches and potato chips," Matt answered before walking over to unstrap the food bundle from Dee's horse.

"That'll do," the man replied.

The next hour was spent eating and listening to the old man ramble on about life on the river and his search for bandit treasure. Matt used all his charm and experience, doing his best to guide the conversation, but getting straight information out of the tattered prospector seemed impossible. The only concrete thing he'd found out was the man's given name—Thomas. He could tell Dee was becoming discouraged. Instead of eating the sandwich she'd unwrapped, she simply pulled pieces from it and nibbled on them.

Finally, when most of the food was gone and Thomas had carefully wrapped the leftovers for his own supper, Matt pushed to his feet and stretched his back.

"Well, I guess we better head on," he said, putting out a hand to help Dee stand. He gazed deeply into her eyes, trying to silently apologize for yet another dead end. Matt was starting to feel helpless and he didn't like it one bit. He'd wanted to give her the one thing he was good at providing, information. She'd roughed it this far through sore feet, snakes and old reprobates. She deserved some answers. But he was no closer than he had been the first day they'd met.

That's when Thomas spoke up. "You know, old Tinker would never hurt a fly. Not since the war."

Both Matt and Dee turned to him. Matt got directly to the point. "Do you know if he ever ran into anyone out here? Someone in trouble or maybe needing directions?"

"It's possible." Thomas cocked his head and gazed at Matt with a surprisingly coherent stare. "But Tinker used to drift in and out back in those days, and he would stay out of sight. Didn't want to talk to nobody."

"Is he different now?" Matt asked, fishing to confirm his suspicion that Thomas and Tinker were one and the same. He knew it was a long shot, but he had questions that needed answers.

He felt Dee go still next to him as if she was holding her breath.

Thomas looked away again, seeing beyond the present. "He talks to me sometimes. He's tellin' me I need to show you somethin'. Somethin' he kept for years waitin' for somebody to claim it."

"What would that be?" Matt asked slowly.

Thomas picked up his dark, polished stick and used it to rise painfully from his seat. Then he looked Dee in the eyes. "Pottery," he said. "Bring your horses and follow me."

He took Matt and Dee back to the abandoned mining shack then made them wait while he dug around at the rear of the ramshackle building. He returned cradling a metal box secured by a rusted piece of wire. With Matt's help, he removed the wire, then with shaking hands, Thomas sat down on a broken chair and opened the box.

Dee gasped when she saw the contents. There had to be thousands of dollars neatly stacked inside, along with rocks streaked with what looked like gold. Thomas pushed aside the money and pulled out a leather pouch about the size of an Indian medicine bag. He lowered the box of money to the ground at his feet and gazed up at Dee before unlacing the bag.

"Hold out your hands," he said.

Dee swallowed once and nervously glanced at Matt. What if the bag was full of spiders or snakes? Or worse, bones? The last thing she wanted to do was to be the first to know. When Matt moved forward as if to take her place, she shook off her fear and held out her hands palms up. She'd wanted to investigate the past—she had to carry it through. She had to know what happened to her father.

Thomas shook the bag and several objects fell into her hands. Almost afraid to look, Dee brought her hands higher and gasped at the sight of what they held. Her heart pounded through several painful beats. On her palms lay four shards of pottery with blue markings, the kind of pottery her father valued the most. The other two objects brought tears to her eyes: a corroded man's watch and a gold wedding band.

She recognized both immediately. With wobbly knees, Dee sank until she was sitting on the ground at Thomas's feet. Reverently, she set the pieces of pottery on the dirt then looked closely at the watch and the ring.

After a moment, Matt squatted next to her and put his arm around her shoulders. "Do these things mean something to you, Dee?"

Dee could only nod because her throat was clogged with emotion. She realized she was crying when one of her tears left a streak of wetness on her upturned palm. With shaking fingers she lifted the wedding ring and scanned the inner surface. She found what she was searching for: the initials D.C. & E.C. Always and Forever. Her father's name was David, her mother's Ellen.

She brought her gaze upward to connect with the old man's. "Where is my father?" she asked hoarsely.

Thomas stretched out a gnarled hand and grasped her shoulder. "I can show you where, but there ain't much to see."

"What happened to him?"

Thomas shook his head sadly and his hand dropped away. "I'm not sure. He must have been out there for months before I run across him. All I can tell you is that one of his legs was busted real bad. Couldn't do nothin' but bury what was left." He withdrew his hand and looked at Matt with a hard gaze. "I didn't kill 'im. I did what we did in country, I took his personal effects for his family and buried him decent."

"Why didn't you tell the law?"

Thomas grimaced and reached down for his metal box. "Who was gonna believe me? Old crazy Tinker. I didn't mind people callin' me that because it made 'em leave me alone. But if they'd come and asked, I would've told 'em." He closed the clasp on the box and began retwisting the wire through it. "If you're gonna take me to jail now, let's git to it."

"I want you to show us where he's buried," Matt said. He helped Dee put the pottery and the watch back in the bag. She took the ring and slipped it on her middle finger for safekeeping. Then he helped her stand and put his arms around her.

"Are you up to this?" he whispered into her hair.

It felt so good to be held. Dee tried to sort through her feelings but was unsuccessful. Sadness, yes, certainly. But no anger. She felt more relieved than anything, yet she knew she needed time to sort through it. She stared at Tinker for several heartbeats. For some reason, she believed him. After all these years, what would be the point of his lying to them? He could have merely sent them on their way without saying a word.

One part of her wanted to stay where she was, in Matt's supporting embrace, but the part of her that needed to know the truth was stronger. She gave Matt's arm a brief squeeze and nodded. "I'm ready," she answered.

13

DEE LEANED BACK on the car seat and closed her eyes. They were driving again, she and Matt. They'd delivered the horses back to Matt's brother's place, and now they were headed west in Matt's car, facing the setting sun. She felt worn-out, completely empty, and strangely, at peace.

True to his word, Tinker had taken them to the spot he said he'd buried her father. There hadn't been much to see, just a patch of ground marked by a pile of stones and two disintegrating pieces of mesquite. But seeing it had somehow ended a quest that had begun eighteen years before. Her father was dead. He hadn't abandoned his family. He'd died doing something he'd loved, hunting relics. Now Dee's mother could understand and go on.

And so could Dee. She turned her head and studied Matt. If she never saw him again, she would probably have dreams about watching him drive. Had she really only known him a week? She'd somehow gotten used to his presence, to his friendship, his help. He'd given her a gift no one else could have offered. He'd healed a wound in her that she'd ignored for years.

Somewhere, during all of that, Dee—up-and-coming, on-air news reporter, ambitious nineties career woman with no time for a man in her life—Cates, realized she'd messed up and fallen in love. With, of all people, Matt Travis, the Lone Star Lover.

The truth seemed to rise through her like a warm caressing current. Love… Now what was she supposed to do about that? She'd been so worried that Matt would get serious about their deal, she hadn't thought about her own feelings, her own vulnerability. Right now, her heart felt expanded, open and lighter than she would have ever imagined. And it was all because of Matt.

"Thank you," she said.

He took his eyes off the road and gazed at her briefly. "You're welcome."

Dee couldn't look away or hide the enormity of what she'd discovered. She loved Ranger Matt Travis. Her very own Mr. Wrong. Telling him would be a huge mistake but she wanted to let him see it in her eyes. Just this once, while she felt new and whole because of him.

"Are you okay?" he asked, frowning.

The low, husky sound of his voice brought back memories of lying in his arms. Dee felt the car slow and knew she had to say something.

"I'm a little tired, but fine. I just want you to know how much I appreciate everything you've done for me."

He relaxed slightly and returned his attention to driving. "Believe me, it was a pleasure. For a while there I thought we were stumped."

Matt seemed to weigh several options before speaking. "Are you too tired to stop by the lake before it gets dark?" he asked.

Dee remembered their first trip to Canyon Lake, under the moonlight, holding on to Matt's steadying arm...wanting him. All her defenses had been intact that night. It had been easy to resist his "aw shucks, ma'am" charm. But now she was in a dangerous mood. The kind of mood that would incite her to follow him anywhere. She didn't have the will to fight her attraction to him right then. And she didn't want to.

"That sounds good," she answered.

THE SUN HAD DROPPED below the horizon by the time Matt maneuvered the car up the steep hill to the park entrance. The sky had gone purplish and the first few stars were visible in the eastern sky as they pulled into the deserted roadside park.

Matt shut off the engine before turning to face Dee. She seemed so different from the woman he'd brought to the lake the first night they'd met. Dressed in khaki pants and an embroidered chambray shirt, with a welcoming expression on her face, Matt could almost forget that she would soon leave him. He decided that for his sanity he would forget it until she reminded him.

He opened his door then walked around the car to open hers. When she offered her hand, he took it and pulled her to her feet. Then he took her mouth in a long slow kiss meant to explain exactly how he felt.

"I've been wantin' to do that all day," he murmured into the nape of her neck.

He felt more than heard Dee's answering sigh of contentment. She seemed exhausted. She rested in his arms as if she never wanted to leave.

"Honey, we need to talk," Matt said into her hair then gently held her away from him so he could look into her eyes. "You have to tell me what you want me to do about your father and old Tinker."

Slowly she gathered herself together to form an answer. "What do you mean?"

"I can make an official report. Have the body exhumed. Make Tinker come in and give a statement. I'll do whatever it takes. Find out whatever you need to know."

Dee started shaking her head before he finished. "No. I don't want you to do that. You've already given me what I need." She shivered slightly. "I can't say why, but I believe him. I think my father got lost and couldn't get back to us." Her eyes welled with tears as she gazed at him then she looked down and twisted the ring on her middle finger. "That's enough. Now I can tell my mother I know the truth."

"Well, if it matters, I think Tinker told us the truth too. He had no motive to kill your father, and he had enough money of his own to run if he had to."

Not knowing what else to say, Matt put his arms around her again. He could feel the beat of her heart against his ribs as she rested. He'd hold her into the next century if she'd let him. Now that he'd completed his part of their bargain, there was no reason for them to be together. And that thought made his chest hurt. How was he going to let her go?

"I want to let it go," Dee said into his shirt. Then he heard her gasp.

Matt's protective instincts went on alert. "What is it?"

"Look," she said.

He turned, shifting her in his arms and gazed out over the water of the lake. A full, harvest moon was rising in the slowly darkening sky.

"It's so beautiful," Dee said.

"I suppose," he said and kissed her again. "But I'd rather look at you." He had to concentrate to keep his tone light. Worrying about losing her wouldn't serve any purpose. He wanted to enjoy their time together, when she was still in his arms.

After another long, mouth-teasing kiss, Dee pushed back slightly and ran shaky fingers through her hair.

"Anyone told you lately that you smell like a horse?"

Matt couldn't hold back his startled laughter. "What?" He grabbed her arms, held her close and noisily sniffed her neck. "You smell a little like old Buddy, yourself," he retorted.

She squirmed, backing away from him, smiling. "Well, I think we both could use a swim to wash away the dust, and the aroma. Are you game?"

Swim? Her words echoed inside Matt. His whole body reacted to the image of the two of them naked, swimming in the clear water together. Dee's skin would be cool and smooth like slick satin and his body would be hot and steaming like an underground geyser ready to blow.

He wasn't sure if one man could stand so much good fortune. But he was certainly willing to give it a try. By the time he wrangled up an answer, Matt's heart was beating double time.

"You bet," he answered, proceeding to lead her across the rocks, down to the narrow strip of smooth sand at the lake's edge.

They undressed each other and waded into the water amid teasing touches and sensual stroking. Things didn't get serious until they were neck deep. Unable to touch the sandy bottom, Dee had to tread water or depend on Matt to hold her up. Without hesitation, she chose Matt.

The power of her trust rolled over his senses like a revelation. Her mouth opened to his and he kissed her hard, trying to hold back the words, but they came out anyhow.

"I love you," he said. When Dee went still in his arms and gazed up at him, he added, "I'm not askin' you to say or do anything. It's just something I need to get off my chest."

Dee watched him for several heart-pounding moments and even in the dim light he could see an assortment of conflicting emotions in her eyes. Not a good sign. He didn't want to discuss it, not now, so he smiled his best carefree grin and challenged her. "Come on, Mz. Dee Cates, let's dance."

Matt didn't wait for her reply. Still smiling, he twirled her around once, then traced the skin of her back with reverent fingers before drawing her close enough to feel her breasts and her sensitive nipples slide against his chest. At her sharp intake of breath, he gradually lifted her high enough to lick and suckle the hard buds, warming them with his lips and tongue.

Whatever comment Dee might have made was lost in a moan. Urgent fingers pushed through Matt's hair to hold on, to guide him closer. He would have sighed in relief if he hadn't been so damn hot for her.

As Matt left her breasts and made another sensual assault on her mouth, Dee felt free, as if she was floating. Not because they were in water, but because Matt held her safe in his arms. *I love you.* She didn't want to think about the fact that she'd almost said the same words back to him. Or about how in the world she would be able to say goodbye to him when the time came. Right now, she only wanted what he wanted—the chemistry. The hot, spontaneous combustion that ignited each time they touched.

She wasn't disappointed. Matt touched and teased, using the buoyancy of the clean lake water to melt all her defenses until she wrapped her legs around him and pleaded for him to push inside her.

Then, as the cool water caressed her back,

Matt's heat filled her—sending, stroking, demanding until, amid groans of pure scintillating pleasure, they both found the heart-stopping explosion they needed.

Dee held on to Matt as she slowly came back to her senses. The night had darkened around them and the moon hung in the sky like a huge, glowing paper lantern. She could feel Matt's every breath, every movement, and she wished— No, wishing wouldn't do them any good. No amount of incredible lovemaking could change things. They'd reached the defining edge of their time together. The day after tomorrow would bring goodbye.

Fighting a growing sense of sadness, Dee grasped at a straw of humor to help her stay in control. She just couldn't talk about love, or leaving. It hurt too much. She kissed the side of Matt's face and spoke into his ear. "We may still smell like horses, but I for one feel *much* better about it."

Matt nuzzled her neck and tightened his arms around her until she thought he wouldn't speak. After letting out a harsh breath, though, he chuckled. "Oh, I just remembered. I forgot to do your hair." With that he held on to her and sank below the surface.

Dee came up sputtering and pushing the weight of her wet hair out of her face. Matt held her until she regained her equilibrium, then she gave him an ineffective shove. "Thanks a lot," she muttered, shivering in the cool water. "Remind me to drown you when I can touch bottom."

"You're welcome." He ran warming hands up her arms. "Are you getting cold?"

"A little," she admitted, not ready to leave the water or Matt just yet. He wrapped his arms around her until her shivering stopped. By then Dee was ready to talk.

"We have to discuss tomorrow night and Sunday."

Matt's features went serious but he nodded. "Let's get dry first," he said. "You stay here for a minute. I've got a pair of sweats in my bag in the car. Let me get those before you get out."

He kissed her once then waded to shore. He dried off using his shirt for a towel, quickly pulled on his jeans and boots and walked up the hill. A few minutes later he returned, carrying a blanket and wearing a clean T-shirt. He met her as she waded out of the water and folded the blanket around her. After helping her dress in her own slacks and his sweatshirt, they walked arm in arm back to the car.

Matt shook out the blanket and draped it over his shoulders before he wrapped his arms around Dee. He had some things to say and he wasn't sure he could do it if he looked in her eyes. He held her against him and leaned back on the car so they were both facing the moonrise over the lake.

"I've decided you don't have to go to my parents' Sunday," Matt said into Dee's ear. He'd decided that he didn't want his family to know Dee, to ask him later if he'd seen her or if they'd managed to get together. How was he supposed to let her go, if everyone else kept bringing her name up?

"What do you mean? Of course I have to go." She tried to rotate in his arms, but he held her steady. His sudden change of plans seemed to catch her off guard. He'd made up his mind though. He'd go with her to the banquet because she'd asked him, but that would be his last night with Dee.

"No, it's just going to be a big hullabaloo. There's no need for you to get in the middle of it. You've had a pretty big week already." His embrace tightened.

"Are you trying to weasel out of going to the banquet? What about our deal?" she asked.

He sighed into her wet hair. "It was a stupid deal. I'm sorry I held you to it so long."

Dee's hands slid over his forearms which were crossed under her chin. "It wasn't stupid," she said. "You found out about my father for me. And after we get this banquet out of the way, I'm going with you Sunday to face your family. Case closed. I owe you at least that much and more." She did manage to turn in his arms this time. As her hands slid around his neck, she brushed her lips against his.

With her soft and willing in his arms, he couldn't think of a damn thing to say that would change her mind. Well, he'd lost the argument, but ended up getting exactly what he wanted—

Dee. "Okay," he answered, trying to sound defeated.

THE NEXT DAY, as Dee drove her car north on Interstate 35, she was beginning to regret asking Matt to come with her. Her original plan to show him how much her job meant to her seemed cruel and childish in light of recent events.

Before leaving, they'd called Dee's mother. First Dee, then Matt had explained what they'd found out concerning her husband's disappearance. After making promises to go home for a visit, Dee had hung up the phone feeling as though a great weight had been lifted from her heart.

Matt had been responsible for that gift. And he'd said he loved her.

She wasn't sure how that could be possible after all the ways she'd tried to discourage him. She knew her faults. She'd always been good at pushing people away emotionally. She relied on things she could control, like her career and her ambition. Distance had kept her focused on her goals and away from the pain and anger over her father's abandonment.

But with Matt, things had been different from the start. He'd slipped past her defenses before she'd been able to put him off with her practiced aloofness. He'd touched her body with fire and soothed her soul by solving the painful puzzle that had been unfinished since childhood.

And he'd given her his heart.

She wished she could accept his love and give hers in return. She wished their lives weren't so complicated and that love could really conquer all. But their sights were aimed in different directions and she didn't know how to change course.

Besides, after tonight, he'd understand the importance of her career. This banquet brought all the elements together nicely. Many of the most influential people in the state would be in the audience. It was the perfect opportunity to make a good impression and therefore gain the credibility so important to a reporter's career. It would bring her one step closer to her goal and one step farther away from Matt.

Tonight would end the fairy tale. Cinderella was going to the ball to lose Prince Charming and she felt like a rat.

MATT GLANCED at his watch. They'd left Dee's hotel at one o'clock. He'd been busy at the office all morning catching up on a few loose ends concerning another case he'd worked on with the San Antonio Police Department. Then he'd packed a bag and picked up the tux. His watch read 2:20 now and traffic was steadily building as they neared the Austin city limits. He wondered how much farther they had to go.

"If you think this traffic is bad, you should see it on a Friday afternoon," Dee commented, following the same line of thought. "In three more exits we can get off the expressway and take surface streets. My place is north of the city, over near the university."

Twenty-five minutes later, they pulled into the driveway of Dee's home. Matt got out of the car and went around to open her door before gazing down the street. It was a new development, with a lot of transplanted trees and well-manicured landscaping. Unlike his own small house in Helotes, a few miles northwest of San Antonio, here there were no toys or dogs cluttering the neighboring yards. No sleepy, small-town streets shaded by huge live oak trees. The homes on this street looked expensive and empty. The perfect cluster neighborhood for young professionals.

He moved to the trunk of the car to retrieve their bags and Dee followed him.

"Are you sure you don't want me to get a hotel room?" he asked as he opened the trunk. He needed to be certain she wanted him here, in her home.

"Don't be silly. I have a guest room, and a huge couch. The choice is yours. It's not like we're strangers."

No, not strangers, he thought. *But not lovers, either. Because lovin' took longer than a weekend. At least the true kind did.* When he didn't smile, she touched his arm and kissed him lightly on the cheek.

"You are welcome here," she said. Then she grabbed her bag and headed for the front door. "But I get first dibs on the shower. Make yourself at home," she added over her shoulder after she let him in.

Matt watched the sway of her hips as she went up the stairs then he closed the door behind him. *Make yourself at home.* Easier said than done. He set down his bag, hung his rented tux on the knob of the entry-closet door then walked through a short hall to the living room. Everything from the off-white carpet to the crystal chandelier over the glass and marble dining-room table looked as though one of those designers had coordinated it. He thought of his own haphazard collection of leather furniture, worn but comfortable. At the very least, he would have to call his home lived-in. Dee's home looked as if she was rarely there.

He heard the sound of water running and realized that Dee must be getting undressed for her shower. Matt decided to check out the rest of the place to occupy his mind. He didn't want to concentrate on the fact that upstairs she was naked and wet...and warm. He already had a real memory of the two of them skinny-dipping in the lake. It wouldn't take much for memory to meld with reality and he'd end up in the shower with her—uninvited. He forced himself to think about a neutral subject—Dee's kitchen rather than Dee.

He opened a cabinet to find a glass, then turned on the faucet. He needed a cool drink of water. In search of ice, he opened the freezer. Just as he'd suspected, there were several neatly stacked boxes of that lean kind of microwave food that women seemed to like. His own freezer had ice cream, a couple of frozen pizzas and a casserole his mother had sent home with him.

He and Dee were as different as day and night, right and left...male and female. Then Matt suddenly realized what they had in common... besides the heat that simmered and flared on the physical side—their careers. They both had jobs they were committed to, and enjoyed.

Matt turned up the glass of cool water and drank it down in a few swallows. This whole thing between them had begun with their careers—Dee interviewing him and him investigating her father's disappearance. But now it looked as if their careers would keep them apart. Unless one of them made a huge sacrifice.

Hell. He didn't want to think about that.

Matt returned to the living room and spent a few minutes perusing her CD collection before he heard the shower shut off. Again his mind wandered. To distract the inevitable images that sprang to mind, Matt fiddled with the stereo and found a country-music station. That way he wouldn't hear every single move she made upstairs.

He'd listened to George Strait and Trisha Yearwood before he heard Dee's footsteps. Wrapped in a thick terry robe that offered tantalizing glimpses of her incredible legs, she moved down the stairs, stopped at the bottom and leaned over the banister.

"The shower is free if you want to go in now."

She had that shy look again, the one he would bet good money not many people saw.

"You have a nice place here," he said, keeping his conversation and his mind off the reason for her sudden shyness, and off the view of her smooth, bare legs.

Dee shrugged and put a hand up to adjust the towel twisted around her wet hair. "Thank you, I think. I bought it furnished and haven't changed it much since I moved in. Like I told you, I stay pretty busy." She waved him forward with her other hand. "Bring your stuff up. The bathroom is off my bedroom. You can take a shower while I do my hair."

Matt had already proven he'd follow Dee anywhere, especially if she intended to lead him to her bedroom. He wanted to see where she slept, where she dreamed so that later, when they'd gone their separate ways, he could lie in his own bed and picture her here. Fuel for fantasies. He shook his head at that erotic thought. What he really needed was to get a life, he thought scornfully. Or to find a way to make a life with Dee.

Her bedroom was different from the rest of the rooms, more homey, more individualized. The wallpaper and curtains matched like everything downstairs. But over the bed there were built-in bookshelves filled with all sorts of books, from hardcover biographies to paperback novels. But before he could ask anything about her tastes, she walked to the open bathroom door and waited for him to follow. She seemed determined to keep a few feet of distance between them at all times.

He stepped closer and watched her get skittish, as if she was standing there naked. He didn't want her to be nervous. He just wanted *her*. "I don't bite, you know." He shrugged and raised his suitcase. "And I've got my hands full."

Dee seemed to relax slightly. "I'm not worried about you," she said, then hesitated before adding, "It's just odd having a man— Having you in my house." In a move meant to change the subject, she self-consciously tugged the towel wrapped around her head and her hair fell free. "I've got to dry my hair," she said abruptly. "The bathroom is free."

Humid air laced with the smell of Dee's shampoo surrounded Matt as he shut the bathroom door and hung his tuxedo on the doorknob. He shook his head in amused disgust—even the smell of her could cause his body to react. Various feminine-looking bottles of cosmetics and lotions were lined up along the steam-blurred mirror. Matt resisted the urge to open one or two and find the particular fragrance he associated with Dee. He'd rather smell it on her skin. The sound of a hair dryer buzzing in the other room interrupted his fascination.

Hell. He was acting like a lovesick schoolboy. If he wanted to smell Dee, he ought to have offered to wash her back when he'd had the chance. Why did the fact that he loved her keep him from acting natural? Standing in her bathroom mooning over her absence wouldn't get him where he wanted to go. He closed the lid of the commode and sat down on it in order to remove his boots. Best to get his mind back to what he'd come in there for—a shower.

AFTER BLOW-DRYING her hair, Dee shut off the dryer and listened to the sound of the shower running. Her impulsive invitation for Matt to accompany her to the banquet was turning out differently than she'd expected. She'd thought that since they'd spent a good part of the last week together, bringing him to Austin wouldn't be a big deal. She'd been wrong. Last night the simple act of him saying he loved her had changed everything between them.

Even though she knew, and *he* knew, they had no future together, bringing him here seemed to elevate their "fling" one step further. And now that he was in her bedroom, in her house, she'd always remember him here. Memories. She'd never forget him. That worried her as much as it comforted.

As Dee combed out her hair and began the process of pinning it up, she wondered what Matt was thinking. He seemed to be as wary as she was. Maybe she was worried for nothing. She'd been clear about her future, and as much as it saddened her, it didn't include being Mz. Right for Mr. Sexy Texas Ranger.

With her disclaimer firmly in place, Dee put the

last pin in her hair and reached for her hair spray. She frowned. She'd left it in the bathroom.

"Are you decent?" Dee asked as she tapped on the bathroom door. The shower had shut off a few minutes before but she didn't want to rush in without warning. The door opened and Matt's face, partially covered by shaving cream appeared before her.

"I guess you could say that," he answered. He opened the door farther and Dee experienced the IMAX view of his broad, damp chest.

Memories of the night before, when they'd wrestled in the cool water of Canyon lake under a full moon, ambushed Dee. Her skin warmed from neck to thigh. "I, uh—I need to get my hair spray."

With a nod, Matt backed up and turned toward the mirror again, giving Dee access to the room. At least he had his tuxedo pants on, she thought in relief. She wasn't ready to share the bathroom with him totally naked. She couldn't help, however, taking advantage of the opportunity to visually map the contours and muscles of his back. To see what she'd only been able to feel as he'd held her.

Suddenly her breath clogged in her throat and without thinking, she put a hand out to touch the palm-size scar below his shoulder blade. She felt the muscles under her fingers tighten. Matt paused between razor strokes and met her gaze in the round fog-cleared glass of the mirror.

"This is where you were shot," she said stupidly. The reality of his nearly being killed hadn't sunk in until this moment.

"Well, that's where the bullet came out," he said matter-of-factly. He touched a small, dime-size scar on his chest. "Went in here, took part of one rib and poked a hole in my lung on the way out."

Unable to stop herself, Dee leaned forward and kissed his shoulder, pressing her hand over the scar as if she could take it away with her touch. "You could have died." *And I would never have known you.*

Matt held her gaze in the mirror as he picked up a towel and wiped the shaving cream from his jaw. He turned and bracketed her face with his warm hands. "I didn't, though," he said as his mouth covered hers.

He kissed her as if he needed to prove how very alive he was. And she wanted that proof. *How in the world am I going to be able to let him go?* her heart whispered. As her hands moved over his chest then around his neck, Dee realized they were going to be late for the rehearsal. When his fingers unfastened the belt to her robe and slipped inside to explore her skin, she decided she didn't care.

14

TWO HOURS LATER, backstage at the historic Driskoll Hotel ballroom, Matt stepped over a tangle of electrical cables and wondered how the stagehands knew what to plug in where. This evening would be a grand production, or so it seemed. A production suited to this fine old hotel.

As technicians tested sound levels and checked the lights, Matt watched the banquet set-up crew place tablecloths and flower centerpieces on more than a hundred tables. He amended his original thought. Tonight would be a *very* grand production. The type of place where Matt had sworn he wouldn't be caught dead.

Dressed in a tuxedo and standing around like he belonged in a store-window display, he felt even further out of his element, the boots and silver-belly Stetson he wore notwithstanding. He'd decided years ago that rubbing elbows with politicians wasn't his style. So what was he doing here?

He ran a hand over his unevenly shaven jaw and remembered—Dee. Less than fifteen minutes before, they had screeched to a halt in front of the hotel, left the car for valet parking and hurried through the Driskoll's stately lobby. Now she was in a hasty meeting with the television crew and he was left on his own to wander and wonder.

He'd rather think about why they'd been late. The nearly wordless, hot joining they'd shared had proved beyond a shadow of a doubt that he was alive. Alive and...kicking. His back still stung slightly from Dee's frantic grip. Now *there* was a memory he didn't mind contemplating.

Somewhere behind him, Matt heard the sound of her voice and it sent a small shock of pleasure through him. As if she'd caught him in his carnal wanderings. He shook his head as he turned in that direction. How in the hell was he supposed to keep a lid on his attraction to her when just the sound of her voice made his heart change rhythm? His body recognized everything about her: her scent, her touch, the sounds she made when he was inside her...

"Matt?" Dee walked toward him along with a harried-looking man with a headset draped around his neck, carrying a bunch of papers. "This is my boss, Jim Delaney. He's the program director for KAUS. Jim, this is Ranger Matt Travis."

Matt extended his hand and the other man shook it briefly as he sized him up.

"You look familiar to me... Have we—" A grin spread across his face and he snapped his fingers. "I know you. You're the Lone Star Lover."

Matt could feel his blood pressure rise. He glanced at Dee. She offered him an apologetic shrug as the man kept on talking.

"We got some great stuff from that party. You're a brave man, facing all those women in one room." He shifted his attention to Dee once more. "By the way, I had Trina go ahead and edit the last piece," he said, referring to her assistant. "We're going to air it a few days earlier than planned."

Dee looked alarmed. Not nearly as alarmed as Matt felt, however. So much had happened between them, he'd pretty well put aside the fact that Dee would be airing her dating-in-the-nineties story. Including his starring role as the Lone Star Lover.

"But I'm not finished." She glanced in Matt's direction. "I've got more audio to go with it."

Jim raised his hands. "Hey, you've been on vacation, remember? Don't worry about it, get the audio to Trina and give her instructions."

An assistant approached them. "We're ready for voice levels and camera check."

Jim indicated for Dee to precede him. "You're going to be terrific tonight. I forgive you for being late." He winked broadly at Matt. "She's one terrific lady."

Dee could have slugged Jim. Not only had he brought up the Lone Star Lover piece, he'd already begun his matchmaking campaign. As she walked to the podium and took her place behind the microphone, she glanced back toward Matt. He was frowning. She wanted to say, *Don't worry, I'll fix this.* But he was too far away, and whatever she said would be picked up by the microphone.

Besides, she had work to do. A contrite smile was the best she could offer him until later. She'd talk to him after the rehearsal, during dinner.

Dee was late to dinner, however. Everyone had been seated and the salads served before she made her way from backstage to her seat next to Matt. Then, when the introductions had proceeded around the table, Dee realized she wouldn't be able to speak to Matt openly. They were seated with, among others, the senior captain from Texas Ranger headquarters in Austin, Daniel Caruthers and his wife.

As she placed her napkin on her lap and picked up her salad fork, Dee leaned toward Matt. "I'm sorry about Jim and the Lone Star thing. I promise to take care of it later."

He simply nodded, then answered a question about San Antonio for Captain Caruthers's wife.

After dessert, the evening became a blur. Comfortable in her emcee capacity, Dee took the stage, made a short welcoming speech, read the governor's introduction without a flaw then turned the podium over to him.

Following the governor's speech, she introduced presenters, congratulated winners and ended the program with the announcement that the guests were invited to stay for music and dancing. By the time Dee made it back into the ballroom, everyone had moved toward the two open bars and the musicians.

It took her a full ten minutes to find Matt. When she did, she stopped in surprise. He was standing with Captain Caruthers, chatting with the governor.

Matt thought if he didn't get out of there quick he might have to fake a heart attack. He'd been slapped on the back and had his hand pumped at least fifty times. It seemed as if most of the people in this room had never met a *real* Texas Ranger before.

And he'd become Captain Caruthers's prize show bull for the duration. It was pretty much the last straw when the governor mentioned that he'd presented Chuck Norris with the key to the city when they'd first begun the TV series "Walker, Texas Ranger."

Not that Matt minded the high opinion these important people seemed to have of the tradition of the Rangers. He had a pretty high opinion of it himself, and did his best to uphold it. But he *did* mind being a Texas Ranger poster boy in a tux.

As the governor shook his hand again, Matt felt a tug on his arm. He turned and realized Dee had found him as the governor spoke to her.

"Well, Miss Cates, you did an excellent job this evening," he said. "I have to say, having an attractive woman on the stage makes the rest of us look a good deal better. Right, Ranger?"

"Yes, sir," Matt agreed, and meant it. Watching Dee, the *professional newswoman*, had certainly been the best part of the evening in his opinion. The only drawback had been seeing just what her career entailed. Where these kinds of affairs tended to make the hair on the back of his neck prickly, Dee seemed completely at ease. She was talented, gracious and beautiful. She deserved to be in the spotlight.

"Thank you, Governor. It was an honor to be here," she replied.

He nodded in acknowledgment. "I look forward to seeing you again next year. Now, if you'll excuse me…"

"Of course," Dee said.

As the governor walked out of earshot, Captain Caruthers slapped Matt on the back. "Son, if you ever had a notion about moving into politics, that's the man to know."

Matt almost shook his head at the irony. Kristen, the woman who'd been intent on marrying him, had tried unsuccessfully for years to bulldoze him in this direction. Dee had gotten him here with a simple invitation and the added opportunity of spending a little more time together.

Time to rein in and get back to reality, Matt decided, before he ended up in a place he'd decided long ago that he didn't want to be. He loved Dee, no question about it. But he knew he couldn't give up everything he'd worked for in order to try to make her happy. And he couldn't ask Dee to give up her dreams either. He just wanted…Dee for as long as he could have her. He turned to her, intending to ask if they could call it a night, but the musicians began playing.

"Daniel?" Captain Caruthers's wife coaxed her husband toward the dance floor. Matt thought he and Dee might actually escape until Mrs. Caruthers gave him a stern, meaningful glance. "Come on, you two," she ordered. "Let's show these people that Texas Rangers can do more than chase criminals."

Matt looked at Dee and she shrugged helplessly. A moment later they were on the dance floor and Dee was in his arms.

She smiled up at him and whispered theatrically, "Alone at last."

"In the middle of three hundred people," Matt added, pointing out the obvious. He felt as though every single pair of eyes in the place watched them dance.

"That's life in the news biz," she said, seemingly unaffected by being the center of attention.

"Don't you mean life in a fishbowl?"

"Oh, come on." Dee laughed. "This isn't so bad. I wouldn't want to do it five nights a week, but surely it's better than a lonely stakeout, or being shot at."

"Personally I'd take either one over this." He pulled his hand from hers and tugged at his collar to emphasize his biggest complaint—the tux. Dee gazed up at him, her blue eyes sparkling, and he forgot his discomfort. He slid his hand back into hers and pulled her closer. "Have I told you how very beautiful you look tonight?"

"Well, no, not since…"

She had that shy look again. The one that made him go jittery all over, making him want to pull her into a dark corner. He knew what the rest of the sentence should have been. *Not since he'd helped her get dressed.* After they'd—

Suddenly, bright light exploded around them. Matt looked up and felt like a deer caught in the headlights of a Mack truck. One of the KAUS cameramen was filming their dance.

"I guess this is where I'm supposed to say 'Act natural,'" Dee said. He glanced down at her, expecting a smile of triumph. Instead, she seemed disgruntled. "I didn't tell them to do this," she added.

"Can you tell them to stop?"

"Not really. Jim probably put them up to it. This is one of those moments when I could say I don't like my job. My personal life is supposed to be off-limits." She stepped closer and rested her chin against the front of his chest. "Sorry. The best thing to do is ignore them. They'll move on in a minute."

Dee sighed in relief when they moved to the governor and his wife. Relaxing in Matt's arms, she felt alternately elated and exhausted. She'd emceed the awards without a hitch and had made several important connections for her future. No wonder Richard, the under-the-weather anchorman, had staked out the governor's banquet for himself all this time.

But, beyond business, the evening had rung a hollow note inside her. She realized what she truly loved was the process of going out into the world, illuminating the lives of the "regular folk" in interviews and feature stories.

Then there was Matt, the man holding her. He'd done so much for her, changed her life in the past week, yet her job had required her to ignore him for most of the evening. She'd never intended to put him on display when she'd invited him here. He'd handled it as well as he seemed to do everything, but she knew he'd be more comfortable in his own world. They were so different, they might as well have come from different species.

The song came to an end.

"Are you free to go yet?" Matt asked as he led her from the dance floor.

Dee brought Matt's arm up to check the time on his watch. "It's ten-thirty. Let's see if we can get out of here without running into someone I know."

THEY ARRIVED BACK at Dee's town house a little after midnight. In the end, they'd had to sneak out of the ballroom like two teenagers giving their chaperons the slip.

As Dee kicked off her shoes inside her front door she felt wrung-out. She wasn't sure she could even make it up the stairs.

"Well, that was certainly an evening to remember," Matt remarked, causing her to glance at him. He'd taken off his jacket before getting in the car. Now his collar was open and his tie dangled around his neck. He looked like a ruffled James Bond, except for the Stetson.

Dee couldn't resist ruffling him further. She removed his hat and kissed him lightly. "Thank you for going with me. I hope it wasn't too painful."

His arms slid around her to keep her close. "No worse than a trip to the dentist," he said. "And at least I can claim to have escorted the prettiest woman in the room."

"Thank you. You looked very handsome yourself." Dee's heart began to pound painfully as she gazed into his smile-crinkled brown eyes and realized she could get used to this. Used to having a lover, a partner, a man like Matt in her life. Someone to come home to.

The very thought precipitated a rush of sobering reality. If she couldn't have Matt, then she didn't want anyone. And she couldn't have Matt. He wasn't the type to be the husband of Ms. Dee Cates, feature reporter. He needed to be Sergeant Matt Travis, Texas Ranger. He'd proved that this evening.

Matt had navigated her world and the people in it, from the governor to her boss, with relative ease. But he'd hated it. He'd been very clear about his aversion to big-city politics and everything it entailed. His job as a Ranger defined his life. He couldn't live in the city and a move to the country would only be a step down for her.

She couldn't love Matt Travis. Not the way he needed to be loved. They were wrong for each other and no amount of wishing, hoping or chemistry would change that fact.

Dee had to work to keep her voice from betraying her thoughts. She also had to begin the process of holding Matt at an emotional arm's length, because tomorrow she had to let him go.

"I put your suitcase in the guest room," she managed to say, and, after a brief moment of silent surprise, Matt's arms loosened. "I don't know about you," Dee babbled on, "but I'm beat." Still carrying his hat, she started up the stairs, expecting him to follow. The sooner she got him settled, the sooner she could retreat to her own room to fall apart.

He didn't follow right away, so she stopped and turned.

"Dee, I—" He frowned and she waited for him to continue. He shook his head slowly and the look in his eyes made her heart hurt. "I think I'll be just fine down here on your couch," Matt said. He stepped forward and held a hand out for his hat. "Don't worry about me."

Dee suddenly felt ashamed, as if she'd slammed the door on the best man she'd ever had the privilege to love. All the joy of a successful evening seemed to drain away. "Are you sure?" she asked.

"Heck, that couch is as big as a boat." Matt smiled halfheartedly. He took his hat from her and tapped it against his thigh. "You go on to bed. We have to get up around sunrise."

Dee watched him walk into the living room, away from her, and the temperature of the air around her felt cooler, lonelier. *This is for the best,* the fearful part of her mind intoned. *If you let him get too close, he'll expect more—a wife, a family.* Dee knew she didn't have more to give right now, and she couldn't afford the price. She'd already invested too much of herself in the deal she'd made with Matt, and she'd lost her heart.

AN HOUR LATER, Matt lay stretched out on Dee's couch in a pair of sweats and a T-shirt, covered by a thin blanket. Comfortable, but wide-awake. He'd finally talked himself into believing that it was just as well Dee had gone to bed by herself. They'd been together almost constantly for a week and she probably needed some time alone. Heck, he could use some time on his own too, he decided.

But on this, their last night together, he'd hoped to hold her one more time. To say goodbye in his own way. To tell her he understood that she couldn't be what he needed and vice versa. Hell. It was probably best this way, to back off and not make a fool of himself.

Then he heard one of the stairs creak.

A moment later, Dee whispered, "Matt? Are you asleep?"

"No, I'm awake," he answered, and raised onto one elbow. "Is something wrong?"

"Not really," she answered as she moved next to the couch. "I can't sleep. Could I lie here with you for a while?"

The hesitant sound of the question made Matt's heart struggle through several hard beats. He couldn't think of a damn thing to say that wouldn't sound idiotic, so he just moved over and lifted the blanket for her to slide in next to him.

Matt knew holding Dee would be a double-edged sword. He figured he'd never get to sleep for wanting to do more. But he was willing to stay awake just to have her warm and trusting in his arms. Funny thing was, though, as soon as he heard Dee's deep even breathing that proved she'd gone to sleep…he drifted off right after her.

15

MATT'S MOTHER met them at the door when they arrived at his parents' house around noon the next day.

Dee felt completely drained. It wasn't because she hadn't slept well the night before. As a matter of fact, she'd slept like a baby, on the couch, in Matt's arms. It was unsettling. After several years of curling up alone in her own cozy bed, why had sleeping on the couch with Matt suddenly become...comfortable?

The memory of Matt kissing and whispering her awake as the first gray light of dawn filtered through the curtains made her toes curl. She smiled in spite of herself. He hadn't been rough or demanding, he'd been...loving. And he'd loved her, slowly and thoroughly, as if he wanted to give her a memory to last a lifetime.

She knew she'd never forget, but even as they'd dressed and made the drive south, Dee knew she wasn't prepared. She wasn't ready to face the reality of leaving Matt.

She and Matt couldn't be long-term anything. Today would be their last day as a couple—real or imaginary.

As Dee took a deep breath and shook Matt's

mother's hand, the woman introduced herself. "My name's Annabelle, but you can call me Belle like everyone else."

On the drive over, Dee and Matt had made a tentative plan to deal with Matt's family. He'd insisted that when the time was right, he would confess the truth. Dee's assignment was to socialize and be congenial until Matt could get his mother aside for a serious talk.

But Dee only had enough time to realize Matt had his mother's eyes before Belle took over. From that moment on, the beginning and the end of Dee and Matt's plan spun out of control like a Texas twister.

The well-kept, old farmhouse was already full of people. In the next several minutes, she was introduced to Matt's two brothers, Nathan, whom she'd met previously, and Christopher, and their wives, one of whom was pregnant, Matt's father, James, and several of the grandchildren who weren't outside playing Frisbee with the dogs.

"Don't worry if you have trouble keeping everyone's name straight or what kids belong to who," Matt said to Dee as he winked at his mother. "Sometimes I lose track myself. I just remember that the teenagers belong to my older brother and the littler ones are Nathan's."

"Well, if you were around more often, you could keep up," his mother replied. "After you two get married and settled, you'll be bringing your own children to join the stampede."

Before Matt could make a comeback, his

brother Nathan called him from the kitchen. "Hey, Matt, come out back. I want to show you my new shotgun."

"Uh…" Matt looked at Dee.

"Oh, you go on," Belle said, patting his shoulder. "Give Dee and I some time to talk about how you met and your plans for the future."

The pained expression on Matt's face would have caused Dee to chuckle if she hadn't been so alarmed by the prospect of entertaining his mother on her own. But before they could save themselves, Dee, along with the other women in the house, were shuffled into the kitchen to talk wedding plans while Matt and most of the men went outside to talk guns.

"I THOUGHT YOU SAID she wasn't comin'," Nathan said out of hearing distance of the other men who were now busy at the barbecue grill.

"I tried to talk her out of it, but she wanted to be here when I told everyone the truth," Matt answered. He looked back toward the kitchen window where he could see Dee seated at the table with the other women. Everyone seemed to be talking at once. He rubbed a hand down his face and shook his head. "Now we're in nose deep and I don't want to rock the boat."

"I guess we better hide my new shotgun after you look at it. I wouldn't want Mom to get her hands on it when your boat sinks."

"Thanks a lot, little brother. Just remember, I intend to mention your part in perpetrating the hoax, when the time comes. And you better swear to everyone that none of this was Dee's fault. Got it?"

Nathan frowned, and looked Matt in the eye. "You really like her, don't you? I mean, I haven't seen you spend so much time and energy on a woman since—"

Matt held up a hand to stop him. "Yeah, I know. Since I almost married Kristen."

"Hmm," Nathan rumbled, and rubbed his chin. "Never liked her much. You have a thing for ambitious city women, huh?"

"Dee is nothing like Kristen." As Matt assured his brother, he realized that he'd spoken the truth. There was a difference between normal ambition and domineering control.

"Well, I hope she can convince Mom of that," Nathan said as the other men caught up with them. "Otherwise, the feathers are gonna fly."

DEE WAS GOOD in front of an audience, she'd proved that hundreds of times. But something about facing the women in Matt's life made her tongue-tied and addle-brained.

"So, Dee. How did you and Matt meet?" Belle asked.

Dee glanced around the table and saw looks of encouragement. It seemed as if everyone wanted to hear the Dee and Matt story. She decided to give it a try, sticking to the truth as much as she could.

"Actually, he's been helping me investigate a

case," Dee answered. *Score one for my side*, Dee decided. *Got out of that one without giving much away*.

"You mean, for the television station?" Matt's pregnant sister-in-law asked.

"Well, not exactly," Dee hedged.

"I didn't think so," Belle spoke up. "When TV cameras come out, Matt usually heads off in the other direction."

What did she say now? Dee couldn't admit she'd followed him around one whole evening helping interview his future mate. She decided the safer course would be to explain about her father. She crossed her fingers. With luck, she could draw the story out until Matt came back.

"It was a personal favor," she began. "You see, my father disappeared in this area when I was twelve years old."

"Oh, how awful!" Matt's other sister-in-law said.

Dee took the ball and ran with it. She told them about how much time they'd spent on Matt's systematic search for leads and how they'd finally found Tinker and her father's grave. By the time she had finished, every woman in the room was teary-eyed. Even Dee felt the power of the story, seeing Matt again as her white knight in a Stetson.

"And in the middle of all that you fell in love," Belle said and squeezed Dee's hand. "Right?"

Gazing into eyes that mirrored Matt's, Dee found she couldn't lie. "Yes, that's right. I— We fell in love."

Belle gave her a quick hug. "Well, you're welcome in our family. I can see why Matt thinks so much of you."

Dee found she couldn't speak, so she only nodded. It was wonderful to be welcomed, even if she couldn't stay. She just wished... *No, don't*, she admonished herself. No use wishing. She had to leave this afternoon and be back at work in the morning. No more detours.

Moving past the emotional moment, Belle pushed to her feet and reached for an apron that rested on the counter. "Well, let's get the rest of dinner on before we have six hungry men lookin' over our shoulders and grumbling," she said.

Each of the women seemed to know exactly what to do. While Belle boiled and peeled what looked like a mountain of potatoes for potato salad, Christopher's wife shucked corn and prepared a pot of fresh green beans. Not having any particular culinary talent, Dee was assigned to help Nathan's pregnant wife make biscuits.

Being put in charge of cutting out the biscuits with a round metal ring made Dee feel like a kid again. In those moments she realized something else about her father's disappearance. Because of it, she'd missed out on normal family functions like helping cook Sunday dinner. With new determination to enjoy the day, Dee soon had flour dust on her hands, her chin and her long skirt.

The sound of the back door opening and men's voices caused her to look around. She met Matt's worried gaze. He looked as if he expected her to be angry or crucified. But as his attention shifted to her chin and the table in front of her, he grinned.

"You look like you've been in a flour explosion," he said, leaning over her to plant a possessive kiss on her cheek. He then handed her a clean dish towel.

Dee snatched the towel out of his hand and thought seriously about popping him with it. But then she realized that every person in the room was watching the two of them. "That's exactly why I'm in charge of biscuit cutting," Dee said with as much dignity as she could muster while wiping her hands and face. "It was something I couldn't burn."

"Now, Dee. Don't be too hard on yourself," Belle said. She gave her son a warning frown. "Nathan's wife could barely boil water when they got married. Isn't that the truth, Jill?"

Jill, the mother-to-be, smiled and nodded her head in agreement. "Leave her alone, Matthew," she warned.

"That's right," Belle said. "Out of my kitchen." She raised an arm like a drill sergeant and pointed to the door. "And that goes for all of you. When dinner's ready, we'll let you know."

As ordered, Nathan and the two teenage boys who'd followed Matt into the room stomped through the kitchen and into the living room. Matt raised his hands in surrender. "Hey, I leave the house for half an hour and the whole family turns against me."

"You're lucky we didn't talk Dee out of having anything to do with you," Jill said, smiling.

Empowered by the approval of the women, Dee made a shooing gesture with her hand. "Out," she said.

Matt shrugged and left.

Whereas Belle was the benevolent ruler of the kitchen, Matt's father, James, ruled the barbecue and the rest of the house. Not by giving orders, but by agreement. Although he didn't say much, Dee noticed that when James did speak, the rest of the family listened. From his sons and daughters-in-law to his grandsons and hopefully, as he put it, his first soon-to-be-delivered granddaughter, everyone in the family appeared to have a great deal of respect for James Travis.

All during a dinner that seemed to take twice as long as any meal she remembered, the adults in the family kept up a teasing banter peppered with friendly rivalry. Dee decided early on to keep out of the line of fire, and by some silent communication the rest of them let her off the hook from most of the teasing. They were relentless with Matt, however—calling him the Lone Ranger and mentioning every kind of trouble he'd gotten into as a boy.

"If you keep this up, I'm gonna go into the living room and sit with the kids. At least they have some respect for their elders," Matt groused.

"Well," James said, taking his time with the word. "Before you go, I'd like to propose a toast to you and Dee." He raised his tea glass and the rest of the family followed his lead. A moment of silence fell over the dining room.

The silence was broken by a child's voice from the other room calling, "Daddy!" A few seconds later one of the younger boys came barreling into the room. "Daddy!" he yelled again then skidded to a stop.

Nathan was already on his feet looking ready to take on anything or anybody. "What is it?" he asked his son.

"Uncle Matt's on TV!"

Dee's dinner suddenly felt like a cold lump of biscuit dough in her stomach. She gave Matt one horrified look before setting down her glass, leaving her chair and heading for the television. The rest of the family filed in behind her with Matt moving up to stand at her side.

Dee's heart began to pound when the anchorwoman at KAUS news announced the last installment of the three part series called "Dating in the Nineties." The children had only seen the trailer—the highlights flashed at the beginning of the newscast to entice the viewer to wait for the whole story.

Now, as the story ran, Dee was forced to watch herself interview Matt, the Lone Star Lover, in living color. Before it was halfway over, Dee's face had warmed considerably and her stomach was churning. Matt's family, gathered around her, were completely silent.

By the end of the piece, Dee had decided to kill her boss. He'd run it a week early and with as much lurid footage as he could include, like Carol Ann's considerable cleavage and close-ups of several women blowing kisses. He'd also run it without giving Dee a chance to add the audio sidebar about Matt's friends pulling a practical joke as she'd promised.

She couldn't look at Matt as the story wound to a close with Matt's friends toasting the Lone Star Lover at the bar. *Okay*, her mind whirled. *I can handle this, I can explain this.* But even as she searched for words, another scene flashed on the screen. A full-length shot of she and Matt dancing at the ball next to the governor and his wife. The image nearly brought tears to her eyes—she and Matt looked so perfect together.

A female voice Dee didn't recognize did the closing for the story. "Now, if any of you ladies are interested in contacting Ranger Matthew Travis aka the Lone Star Lover, you can reach him through *Texas Men Magazine*."

The station went to a commercial and Dee swallowed to ease the growing ache in her throat. Not only had she failed to get the practical-joke disclaimer added, but now, because of her, the whole setup had gone from *Texas Men Magazine* to network TV. If Matt thought he'd had too much attention before, he was doomed now. What were they going to tell his family? Dee's worst fears were realized when Belle spoke.

"What was all that about?"

Then everyone started talking at once. Dee wanted to put her hands over her ears and scream but that would only make her look as if she was losing it—although she was close. She turned to face them and the noise died down.

"I'm sorry," she said to the room. Then to Matt she added, "I am so sorry."

He grasped her arm as if she might fall if he didn't hold on to her. "Dee—"

She shook her head and met his gaze. "It's time you told them the truth," she said. Then, using every ounce of her professional control to keep the tears in her burning eyes from falling, she walked out of the room and out of the house.

MATT FOUND Dee out near the barn ten minutes later. She was leaning against a fence absently running a consoling hand over the neck of the old pinto pony the kids usually rode. He leaned on the fence next to her and propped a boot on the lowest railing, but she didn't acknowledge him. Every line of her body looked defensive.

"You need to watch old Petey there," Matt warned, trying to lighten her mood a little. "He bites."

His own mood wasn't faring so well, either. Earlier, he'd been the one ready to bite. But he'd gotten over it, and he figured his family would too. And it bothered him to see Dee so upset.

"It wasn't your fault," he said.

"Yes it was," she answered and finally looked at him. Her eyes were red as if she'd been crying, yet her composure was cool.

"My mother is already planning on a lynching

party for Bill Hazard, and my brother is in the dog's outhouse for helpin' him."

Dee shook her head, her feelings obviously unchanged. "You want to know why it's my fault?" she asked.

Matt knew a loaded question when he heard one. He groped momentarily with the idea of distracting her but gave up finally and stepped into the line of fire. "Okay, why is it your fault?"

She crossed her arms over her breasts as if to put even more space between them before she answered. "Because I didn't do my job."

"What?"

"I know that Jim put that piece together and made the decision to run it early," she said. "And I intend to give him hell for it." She blinked and looked away for a second then returned to finish. "But the real reason the story appeared like it did was because I was too busy with you to take care of my work."

Matt's dander rose slightly. "So, it's *my* fault?"

"No." She loosened her arms and ran a shaky hand through her hair. "It's mine." The bleak look in her eyes made Matt's throat hurt. "I know better than to mix business with…my personal life. But I did it anyway and look what happened."

Matt tried to speak but she put a hand to his lips and stopped him.

"I love my job and I didn't get this far by not giving it all my attention. I'm just sorry you were hurt by my lapse in professionalism." Her hand fell away, allowing him to speak.

"I'm not interested in your professionalism," Matt responded before thinking.

"I see." Dee drew herself up. "Well, that's who I am. That's what I am."

"Hold on." He reached for her. "I didn't mean it that way." He'd meant to say he *was* interested in her personal life, but he'd blown it. She stepped away from his outstretched hand.

"It's time for me to go back to my life and my job. Our deal is over. I'm sorry you got the raunchy end of it."

"Dee—"

She shook her head. "Please take me back to my car," she asked. "I want to go home."

LATER THAT EVENING, when Dee was back in Austin, curled up alone in her own bed, she decided that her last conversation with Matt might have been her best professional performance ever. She'd managed to leave him without breaking down, without telling him how much she wanted to stay...how much she loved him. Then she'd cried all the way home.

Damn.

She missed him already.

Tomorrow will be better, she chanted, searching to find comfort in something. First thing in the morning she would report to the job she loved. The job that had introduced her to Matt and had taken him away at the same time. Then things would get back to normal.

Dee's eyes filled with tears again so she closed them. She'd feel better in the morning, she promised herself one more time. Especially after she'd told Jim where to stuff that story he'd edited then put her name on. Matt, the dependable one, had done everything to fulfill his part of their bargain, and she'd failed to live up to her word. That wasn't like her, and she was determined to fix it.

Damn.

16

MATT SLUMPED BACK in his chair and propped his boots on the edge of the desk. He'd thought that his life had reached an all-time record low a week before when he'd walked into the Hole in the Wall bar and found himself a sex symbol. But that had been nothing compared to how depressed he felt now.

He missed the hell out of Dee, her smile, her smell, the small of her back... She'd only been gone five days—well, technically four and a half.

And his phone wouldn't stop ringing. Most of the women who'd been at the bar that night had called again, mixed in with a few more who'd seen him on TV. He'd been asked to do interviews by the local papers and television stations as far away as Dallas. He'd even gotten a message to call Captain Caruthers in Austin. Everybody but God and the governor had telephoned him.

Everybody except Dee.

Matt rubbed a hand down his face and straightened his shoulders. He was determined not to take Dee's leaving personally. Sure, he'd fallen in love with her, but he'd known all along that they couldn't be together. Besides, she'd never said she loved him. Not out loud, anyway.

If she can walk away, she isn't the right woman, his pride whispered. But his heart knew there was more to it than that. Finding her father hadn't changed the fact that she was afraid of trusting a man, of depending on a man. So her career had become her lover, her safe haven.

Not so different from his own career, he realized. He'd been pretty self-contained over the years, never getting too close to any woman. Set in his ways. Then Dee had walked into his life, had gotten under his skin and touched his heart before he understood what was happening.

Hell.

Matt pulled his hat down low and closed his eyes. He was getting good at sliding back through the memories of holding Dee, laughing with her...loving her. That was the only way he could get through the pain of missing her—that and working. Keeping busy seemed to help, although even then sometimes he could hardly breathe for the tightness in his chest.

Without warning the door of his office swung open and hit the wall. Matt opened his eyes. Bill Hazard stood on the other side of the desk.

"Don't make me shoot you," Matt threatened without moving a muscle.

"You takin' to sleepin' in your office these days?" Bill said.

"That's none of your business," Matt answered.

Bill balanced his hands on his hips and scowled. "Because of me, there are women all over this town lookin' for you. If I'd known you were gonna be so grumpy and uncooperative, I'd have picked someone else to be the Lone Star Lover."

Matt figured that was about the closest he would ever get from Bill in the way of an apology. But he wasn't ready to accept it yet so he remained silent.

"What do I have to do to get you back to normal? Kidnap that TV lady from Austin and bring her back?"

Matt didn't realize he was mad until his boots hit the floor and he stood up. "Her name is Dee Cates and you aren't going to do a damn thing to her. Understand?"

Bill put a hand up in surrender and took a step back. "Okay, okay. See what I mean about grumpy?" He sighed and scratched his head. "If you'll just tell me how to get your mother off my case, I'll leave you alone."

A smile rose inside Matt. His mother could be a hellcat when protecting her family. "You should have thought of that before you started all this," Matt said emphatically.

"Yeah, I know hindsight is twenty-twenty, but—"

The ringing of the phone interrupted him. Matt reached for the receiver wishing he could just yank the cord from the wall instead of answering it. His mother's voice greeted him.

"Hi, Mom," he replied, giving Bill a wicked smirk.

Bill groaned and sat down in the chair opposite the desk.

"What?" Matt had to ask his mother to repeat her statement because he couldn't believe his ears.

"I said, Dee Cates called. She asked me to round up the family and have them watch the Sunday-afternoon news. She also said to invite Bill Hazard and those other overgrown children who pulled the joke."

Matt wanted to ask if she and Dee had talked about him at all, but he couldn't do it in front of Bill. And his mother seemed unwilling to elaborate.

"Okay. Bill's here in my office, I'll tell him. 'Bye."

Bill's uncomfortable look almost made Matt smile. But the fact that Dee had called his mother instead of calling him had taken all the pleasure out of torturing his so-called friend.

"You're invited to Sunday dinner," Matt said tersely.

"Oh no, I can't. I have to go—"

"I'd advise you to be there, old friend. Or my mother will call Rayanne and— Well, you know how that could end up."

"All right, we'll be there," he said reluctantly. "She, uh, wouldn't poison me or anything, would she?" Bill looked as though he was only half kidding.

"No," Matt answered, but before Bill got too comfortable he added, "Mom prefers guns."

As DEE PUT the finishing touches on her notes for the Sunday newscast, there was a knock at the door.

"Come in."

Jim stuck his head in the opening. "We have about five minutes to air," he said.

"Fine," Dee answered, going back to her notes.

Instead of leaving, Jim leaned against the door frame, his hand on the knob. "You don't have to do this, you know."

Dee looked at him again. "Yes, I do," she answered. Case closed as far as she was concerned. "I owe him— No, *we* owe him that much," she added.

"All right, but don't forget I told you so. Risking your career isn't the answer."

Her career was the only thing she had to risk. She'd already lost her heart to Matt. And lately, her career hadn't felt like enough. "It's my decision," she said, ending the conversation.

She didn't feel like talking. Each time she read through her prepared speech, her eyes got teary and her voice wobbled. It would serve her right to be humiliated on the air. After what they'd done to Matt— No, what *she'd* done to him, she had to at least try to apologize.

This week had been hell. Everything had been one step ahead or one step behind. Nothing was flowing smoothly anymore, not her work, and certainly not her life. Just that morning her faithful assistant, Trina, had finally threatened to quit if Dee didn't at least talk to her two or three times a day.

The only person she wanted to talk to was Matt. But she couldn't bring herself to do that, not one-on-one. What would she say? *Gee, I love you but I can't live with you because of my job?* She'd been asking herself questions all week without discovering any new answers. She'd run out of ideas. She looked at her watch. She'd run out of time, too.

Dee organized her notes and pushed her hair into place. *Well, here goes nothing…here goes everything.*

MATT SAT DOWN on the couch with a beer balanced on his knee. True to Dee's request, his mother had gathered the whole family along with the instigators of the joke. And, up to this point, she hadn't killed anyone.

Matt watched the liquid in the half-empty bottle of beer in his hand slosh around and realized he was anxiously tapping his foot. Damn. He'd halfheartedly asked for the beer to keep his hands busy, but there wasn't much he could do with his feet.

He was nervous as hell—like a long-tailed cat in a roomful of rocking chairs. He remembered all too well the last broadcast they'd witnessed together. Today might be even worse. He had no idea what to expect. But if Dee asked them to watch, then by God, they'd watch. Before he could draw in a calming breath, he was looking at Dee's face, in living color on the television screen.

"Good evening," she said.

Matt's heart did several gymnastic tumbles at the sight of her beautiful face and the sound of her smoky voice.

"Last week we ran a story that I researched on dating in the nineties. I'm here this evening to make a Texas-size apology and to set the record straight. The facts of the story were both sensationalized, and in one particular instance, very wrong.

"Since it was my story and my responsibility, I would like to take this opportunity to correct these errors."

Matt listened in amazement as Dee went on to explain the practical joke before announcing that he was not the Lone Star Lover.

"Finally—" Dee's voice broke and she blinked several times before continuing. "I would like to personally apologize to Ranger Matt Travis and his entire family for all the discomfort this story has caused them. I hope you can find it in your hearts to forgive me. Thank you, good night."

Matt wanted to take a sip of beer to clear his throat but he knew he wouldn't be able to swallow. Dee had gone on TV and risked the thing that mattered most to her, her credibility as a reporter and her career—just to apologize to him. She had to love him, whether she knew it or not.

The weather news followed Dee's emotional broadcast and Matt's father turned off the TV in midforecast. Unlike the last time they'd been in the same room all talking at once, now the room was silent.

"Well?" his father finally said. "Matthew? Didn't you tell me that the captain offered you a job in Austin?"

"The job is actually in San Angelo, thirty miles—"

His father interrupted him by raising a few fingers toward the television set. "What are you going to do about this?"

"What do you mean?" Matt replied.

"About Dee. Do you love her?"

"Yes, sir," Matt answered, unwilling to lie.

"Seems to me, then, that it's time you went after her. I didn't raise you up to be a quitter."

"Yes, sir." Matt said and smiled for the first time since Dee had left.

BY MONDAY MORNING, things had gone from rocky to crazy for Dee. She'd been called into the station manager's office for a meeting about her newly altered public image. She'd gotten calls from two affiliates offering her jobs, and her assistant was taking great glee in announcing the results of the ongoing public-opinion lines run by the station.

Instead of hurting her career, her confession had actually boosted both the station's ratings, as well as her own.

Unfortunately, Dee found no personal satisfaction in her public apology. All that mattered was that Matt Travis was out of reach and out of communication. She'd called him two times and paged him once. She'd wanted to say in person what she'd said on television. And she'd wanted to talk to him, to hear his voice.

But he hadn't returned her calls.

She didn't blame him. After all she'd put him through... She sighed and tried to concentrate on the tape she'd been editing for the last thirty minutes. She needed at least ten seconds of good footage.

Trina bustled through the door, interrupting her wavering attention span once more.

"Got a tape from the San Antonio affiliate," she said, casually tossing the tape on the desk in front of Dee.

"I'll look at it in a minute, I have to—"

"It was hand-delivered. I think you better check it out," Trina insisted.

As Dee crossed the small office and slid the tape into a playback unit, she heard voices and people shushing each other behind her. She turned and saw that the tiny space was filling up with her co-workers.

"What is this? My birthday?" Dee asked and then she heard Matt's voice coming from the television.

"Hello, Dee," he said.

A spontaneous thrill of excitement ran through her. With a pounding heart, she turned to the screen and saw his face.

"I wanted to thank you for what you did on

Sunday. I appreciate being off the hook Bill had hung me on." Matt rubbed a hand down his face and pushed his hat back a little.

The familiar gesture brought tears to Dee's eyes.

"There's one other thing I want to do and I decided that if I'm gonna' be a fool, I might as well be on TV when I do it," he said.

The room around her had gone deadly quiet and Dee found she could barely breathe. She brought one trembling hand up to her throat.

Matt grinned, and Dee had to blink away tears. "I love you," he said. "I know, I told you that before, but this time I want to add somethin'. I've accepted a job in San Angelo and I want to know if you'll marry me. That way we can both have our careers, each other and everything else.

"Please think about it. Oh, and by the way, if you don't marry me, this tape will self-destruct in five seconds." He winked at her as the VCR image faded to black.

Dee didn't want to turn around and face the people behind her but she had no choice. All she could think of was getting back to Matt, to feel his strength, his warmth, his lips.

"Trina, I need a telephone," she said. People moved back out of her way as she reached to open the door. When she opened it, Matt was standing on the other side.

For two heartbeats, they stared at each other, then Matt opened his arms.

"So, what do you say?" he asked.

"I do love you," Dee confessed as he folded her in his embrace. She gazed up into his eyes and added, "The answer is yes, yes, and definitely yes." Then she laughed. "I can't believe I'm going to marry the Lone Star Lover."

A round of whoops and applause broke out from the people around them. As Matt kissed her, Dee heard Jim's voice, her boss, bellow over the din.

"Finally!"

_____ Epilogue _____

Two months later

"WELL, that ends our local news for this evening," Richard, the KAUS anchorman, said. "But we have one more item on our broadcast-family front. The station would like to announce that our very own feature news reporter, Dee Cates, was married today here in Austin."

The screen filled with a full-length shot of the bride and groom leaving the church among family and well-wishers.

"It seems that while researching a story on dating in the nineties a few months back, Dee found her own Mr. Right, Ranger Matt Travis of San Antonio. We here at KAUS extend our heartfelt congratulations to the happy couple.

"Good night."

HARLEQUIN® *Temptation*

He's strong. He's sexy.
He's up for grabs!

Harlequin Temptation and
Texas Men magazine present:

1998 Mail Order Men

#691 THE LONE WOLF
by Sandy Steen—July 1998

#695 SINGLE IN THE SADDLE
by Vicki Lewis Thompson—August 1998

#699 SINGLE SHERIFF SEEKS...
by Jo Leigh—September 1998

#703 STILL HITCHED, COWBOY
by Leandra Logan—October 1998

#707 TALL, DARK AND RECKLESS
by Lyn Ellis—November 1998

#711 MR. DECEMBER
by Heather MacAllister—December 1998

Mail Order Men—
Satisfaction Guaranteed!

Available wherever Harlequin books are sold.

HARLEQUIN®
Makes any time special ™

MEN at WORK

All work and no play?
Not these men!

October 1998
SOUND OF SUMMER by Annette Broadrick

Secret agent Adam Conroy's seductive gaze
could hypnotize a woman's heart. But it was
Selena Stanford's body that needed saving—
when she stumbled into the middle of an
espionage ring and forced Adam out of
hiding....

November 1998
GLASS HOUSES by Anne Stuart

Billionaire Michael Dubrovnik never lost a
negotiation—until Laura de Kelsey Winston
changed the boardroom rules. He might
acquire her business...but a kiss would cost
him his heart....

December 1998
FIT TO BE TIED by Joan Johnston

Matthew Benson had a way with words
and women—but he refused to be tied
down. Could Jennifer Smith get him to
retract his scathing review of her art by
trying another tactic: tying him *up?*

Available at your favorite retail outlet!

MEN AT WORK™

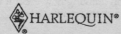 

COMING NEXT MONTH